A Degrassi Book

Snake

Susin Nielsen

James Lorimer & Company, Publishers
Toronto, 1991

Copyright ©1991 by Playing With Time Inc.

All rights reserved. No part of this book may be reproduced or transmitted in any form, or by any means, electronic or mechanical, including photocopying, or by any information storage and retrieval system, without permission in writing from the publisher.

Cover photo: Janet Webb

Canadian Cataloguing in Publication Data
Nielsen, Susin, 1964 -
  Snake

(Degrassi ; 18)
ISBN 1-55028-370-7 (bound)
ISBN 1-55028-368-5 (pbk.)

I. Title. II. Series

PS8577.I45S5 1991   jC813' .54
C92-093186-3
PZ7.N54Sn 1991

James Lorimer & Company, Publishers
Egerton Ryerson Memorial Building
35 Britain Street
Toronto, Ontario
M5A 1R7

Printed in Canada

This book is based on characters and stories from the television series *Degrassi Junior High/Degrassi High*. This series was created by Linda Schuyler and Kit Hood for Playing With Time Inc., with Yan Moore as supervising writer.

About the Author

Susin Nielsen graduated from Ryerson in 1985 with a degree in Radio and Television Arts. Since then she has written sixteen episodes of the award-winning series, "Degrassi Junior High" and "Degrassi High." *Snake* is her fourth Degrassi book.

Susin lives in Toronto with her husband, Goran, and their two fat cats, Lucy and Mr. Mooney.

Degrassi Books
based on the Degrasssi Junior High/
Degrassi High TV Series

Exit Stage Left by *William Pasnak*
Stephanie Kaye by *Ken Roberts*
Spike by by *Loretta Castellarin*
Shane by *Susin Nielsen*
Melanie by *Susin Nielsen*
Joey Jeremiah by *Kathryn Ellis*
Lucy by *Nazneen Sadiq*
Caitlin by *Catherine Dunphy*
Wheels by *Susin Nielson*
Snake by *Susin Nielson*
BLT by *Cathy Dunphy*
Maya by *Kathryn Ellis*

Chapter 1

Thwap, thwap, thwap. Thwap, thwap, thwap. Snake dribbled the basketball up and down the court, trying to keep the ball as low as possible, trying to concentrate only on his hands and his feet. Control, he told himself over and over. Just stay in control.

The coach liked that word. "If you have control," he'd said at the last two practices, "not just over the ball but over your mind and your body, you can't lose." Some of the guys made fun of Coach Singleton's advice because they thought it sounded spacey, but Snake felt he understood. Out on the court, it *was* possible to have complete control. Snake knew. It had happened to him a couple of times. It never lasted long; sometimes it was only a few beautiful seconds before someone snatched the ball away or until he lost his concentration. But while it lasted, it felt sensational. He knew it took lots of practice. But at least it was a goal he could work toward. At least it was possible.

If only it could be that way in life, he thought now as he leaped into the air, the ball held high over his head, his body arching before he dunked the ball expertly into the hoop. If only all it took was lots of practice to have control over his life. But that wasn't the way things worked. There were too many outside factors, too many unknowns, too many surprises waiting to pounce at him from behind every corner. It wasn't fair. Just when he'd started to make sense of ninth grade, one of those nasty surprises had to land right in his lap.

Snake looked at the clock that hung high on the far wall in the gym. Eight-thirty. He had another half hour before school started. Usually, he didn't get to school until the last minute and he'd have to sprint down the hall to make homeroom on time. He wasn't a morning person.

But this morning had been different. He wasn't able to sleep, so at six o'clock, he quietly slipped into his clothes, grabbed his gym bag and school books and tiptoed out of the house without eating breakfast. He walked all the way down to the Beaches and strode up and down the boardwalk for over an hour before turning back and heading to school.

Snake thought about something else Coach Singleton had said to them last Friday, when they'd had their first practice as the Degrassi Junior Boys' Basketball Team. "Remember, being on a team is like being part of a large family. You'll probably have some arguments, disagreements — just like families do. But you must be loyal and supportive of every member of this family. If someone at home has a problem or falls ill, what happens? The whole family rallies around that person to help. It should be the same here. Otherwise, the family — this team — will fall apart."

At the time, Snake got the message loud and clear. But now, as he mulled over the coach's words, he thought the message was too simplistic. What did you do when a family member hit the rest of you with such horrible news it was like you'd had the wind knocked out? With something so horrible you'd never, *ever* be able to "rally around that person"?

Snake tossed the ball toward the hoop, but this time he missed by a long shot. He knew what the answer was.

The family would fall apart.

But that wasn't always the family's fault. Sometimes you *could* dump all the blame on just one person.

Thwap, thwap, thwap. Snake started to dribble fast and furious down the court, his teeth grinding together and his breathing getting heavy. He was exhausted. He knew he should stop, but he couldn't. He threw the ball toward the hoop again. Again, he missed. "Cripes," he said under his breath, retrieving the ball and starting over again. Sometimes he couldn't believe he'd made the team. He would have to play better than this if he didn't want to be booted out after their first game.

He wanted to play so badly. He'd never been very good at sports, but because of his brother, he'd always dreamed of making the Degrassi basketball team.

When he thought back to last year's tryouts, he cringed. He'd been awful. When he found out he hadn't even made the first cut, he felt humiliated. Like a big fat zero. He remembered what his brother had said when he phoned him at his university residence that night.

"When I'm home next summer, I'll teach you everything I know. They'll be dying to have you on their team next year."

Glenn kept his promise. During the summer, they played almost every day. At first, Snake didn't feel he was getting any better; then one day, he made a breakthrough. All the stuff Glenn taught him seemed to come together, and Snake finally felt like he understood the game of basketball.

When he saw his name on the team list last week, he felt ecstatic. The first thought that crossed his mind was to phone Glenn. But when he tried to phone his brother at the dorm that night, he wasn't there. So he tried the next night. And the next.

"He's still not here," a voice said on the other end of the line.

"Do you have any idea where he might be?"

"Nope."

Yesterday, after their second gruelling practice, Snake left the gym with some of his teammates. By now, they all knew who his brother was, because Glenn's photo still hung in the hall outside the change-rooms, along with all the other photos of kids who'd won sports awards over the years at Degrassi. When Glenn was at the school, he was voted Most Valuable Player on the basketball team two years running.

"He obviously got all the talent in your family," Luke joked as they walked toward the exit together.

"Ha, ha," Snake replied. But in a way, it was true. The things that Snake struggled with always came easily to Glenn. He always had top grades at school. He was always a good athlete. Everything Glenn touched turned to gold.

To top it off, he was a good brother. He was always there when Snake needed him. Until yesterday, Snake had wanted to be exactly like him. "Obviously he got the looks, too," Bryant Lester Thomas, better known as BLT, said, glancing at the photo as they strolled past.

"Since when are you so interested in my looks?" Snake shot back.

BLT made his wrist go limp and started to prance around the foyer. "Since I decided I was a homo," he said in a high-pitched voice. The guys burst into laughter as they left the school.

"If I wasn't already seeing Luke," Snake said, throwing his arm casually around Luke's shoulders and lisping, as they stood on the front steps, "I'd sure like a chance to get to know you better."

Luke spun out of Snake's arm and slugged him. "Get away from me, you fag!" he shouted in mock horror.

Suddenly a voice called out from the parking lot. "Hey, Archie!"

Snake turned around. Only his family called him by his christened name. In the parking lot, he saw a sleek black Jeep with the top down, even though it was late October. Inside the Jeep sat Glenn. His brother.

"Man, look at those wheels," BLT whistled.

"Come on," Glenn called. "I'll drive you home."

"Can we get a ride?" Luke pleaded.

"Sorry, guys," Snake replied as he headed toward the parking lot, a grin on his face. "Maybe another time."

"Where have you been?" he shouted as he hopped into the Jeep beside his brother. "I've been trying to phone you. I made the team."

Glenn started to laugh. "Way to go, Arch." He grabbed him and gave him a bear hug. "That's great news."

"So, why aren't you in school? Don't you have classes?"

"Classes got cancelled for a couple of days," Glenn answered with a tight-lipped smile.

Something in Glenn's voice made Snake feel uneasy. "You haven't dropped out, have you?"

"No. I like my courses. I still want to be a doctor. And my marks are just fine."

"Oh, man, it is *so* great to see you," he said. Glenn had left home over a year ago to start university, but Snake still missed him. The house felt too big, too quiet, without him there.

In a few minutes they arrived home. Home was a large, well-kept, and comfortable old house in Toronto's east end. A car was in the driveway. When Glenn shut off the ignition, Snake started to jump out of the car. "Mom's home. She's going to be so surprised."

But Glenn grabbed Snake's arm. "Wait."

Snake sat back down in the passenger seat. So he was right. Something was wrong. "What?"

"Classes weren't cancelled. That's not why I'm home. The reason I came home is to tell Mom and Dad ... and you ... I'm moving out of the dorm."

"Yeah?" Snake shrugged.

"Yeah, into a nice apartment in downtown London with a good friend. We have so much in common. And there's a lot of things we want to do together. Someone I care for very much."

Suddenly it dawned on Snake. He broke into a grin and slapped his brother on the shoulder. "Oh, I get it. You're moving in with a girl, right? Well, Mom and Dad won't like it, but they'll get used to it."

"No. It's a guy. His name's Greg."

"So?"

"He's gay."

Snake grimaced. A fag? His brother, sharing a bathroom, plates, a TV set? Being forced to *talk* to — a fag? This, he knew, would not go over well with their parents. "What are you moving in with one of those for?"

"I'm gay, too."

At first, Snake smiled. "You're joking, right?"

But Glenn didn't smile back.

Snake just stared at his brother, then at anything *but* his brother. Before either of them had a chance to say anything else, their mother appeared at the doorway.

"Glenn! I thought I heard you. What are you doing home? Come on in!" She approached the Jeep, arms outstretched.

"I hope you can understand," Glenn said in a low whisper to Snake before hopping out of the Jeep to hug their mother.

Snake just remained where he was, sitting dazed in the passenger seat of the car as his brother and mom entered the house. What? *What??*

He sat there until his mom opened the door again. "Archie Simpson, what do you think you're doing, just sitting there? You'll catch a cold. Come in and talk to your brother."

So he'd gone in. But he hadn't said a word to Glenn. And the evening had gone from bad to worse.

Snake whipped the basketball as hard as he could against the wall as the five-minute warning bell rang. *"Whack!"*

Glenn's words rang in his ears. "I hope

you can understand."

He didn't understand, he told himself as he walked to the changeroom. He didn't understand at all.

Chapter 2

The next morning, Snake lay in bed, still drowsy, the covers pulled up around his chin. He'd hardly slept again, and he wished he could just stay in bed. Through the window, he could see it was a cold, grey autumn day, and that made him want to stay in bed even more.

He was jolted fully awake by a knock at his door. "Archie, get up," his dad's voice boomed through the door. His dad had one of those voices that, even when he was whispering, seemed to carry for miles. "You'll be late for school."

"Okay, okay," Snake mumbled back.

"I'm running late. I'll see you tonight."

That was one load off his mind, thought Snake. The idea of having breakfast with his parents made his stomach churn. Two days had passed since Glenn's visit, but they still hadn't talked about what happened.

He dragged himself out from beneath the covers and shuffled over to his drawers to get a clean pair of underwear and a T-shirt.

As he passed the mirror that hung over the bureau, he caught a glimpse of himself and groaned. What a sight. At fourteen years old, Snake was already six feet tall. Some guys would think his height was an asset, but Snake didn't think so. It would be different if he had the body to go with it. He stared at his scrawny, pale frame and sighed. Freckles covered almost every inch of his skin, and his hair was orange. His mother called it "strawberry blond," but Snake knew orange when he saw it.

Snake was sure BLT was only half-joking when he said Glenn got all the looks in the family. The only similarity between the two brothers was their height. When Glenn was Snake's age, he was just as tall, but his body was toned and muscular, his skin bronzed and freckle-free, his hair dark brown and wavy.

The phone seemed to ring constantly when Glenn was in high school. Snake remembered his mom calling upstairs, "Glenn, it's Irene," or "Glenn, it's Andrea," or "Glenn, it's Janice."

"You've certainly got a way with the women," their dad would say to Glenn, shaking his head. "I wish I could take the credit, but you sure didn't learn it from me."

Snake turned away from the mirror. How ironic. If only he could have half the luck Glenn had had with girls.

It wasn't just his looks, either. Glenn was charming. Considerate. Funny. Outgoing. Snake, on the other hand, was shy. Awkward. And not at all outgoing. He remembered how he and Joey and Wheels had dreamed last year about being in ninth grade, the year that they were supposed to be the Kings of the Castle. But here he was, in grade nine at last, and it hadn't made much difference. Sure, he'd made the basketball team, but aside from that, all grade nine had offered him so far was more confusion.

His mom called him "sensitive." "Archie's always been the sensitive one," she'd say.

Boy, how Snake hated that word! "Don't call me that," he snapped at her last time she said it.

"But Archie, it's a compliment. There's nothing wrong with being sensitive."

Right. Easy for his mother to say. At least his mom had the common sense not to call him "The Sensitive One" when his friends were around.

The worst of it was, he knew his mom was right. When he was growing up, Snake had never joined the rough games the guys played, preferring to read or play with the girls. He couldn't stand seeing cruelty of any kind. He remembered running home in tears one day because a kid in his neighbourhood convinced Snake to catch flies with him, telling him they could study them like a science experiment. But once they were caught, the kid proceeded to pluck off their wings one by one.

Now, at fourteen, he still couldn't stand to see someone being picked on. And if anyone insulted him or made fun of him, he hurt for days.

Let's face it, he said to himself now. You're a wimp.

Snake found some clean clothes and slipped into them. He took his time, not wanting to leave his room until his father left. When he heard the door slam, he grabbed his gym bag and headed downstairs.

At lunchtime, Snake wound his way through the cafeteria, keeping his eyes peeled for his friends. It was crowded with seventh-, eighth-, and ninth-graders. Some of the kids had been angry last year when the principal had announced that a ninth grade would be attached to Degrassi Junior High, because they'd been dying to go to a real high school. But Snake hadn't minded too much. In fact, he'd been kind of relieved. At least he felt at home here.

"Hey, Wheels. Do we know that guy?"

"Gee, I don't know, Joey ... The freckles look oddly familiar."

"Very funny," Snake said, plopping down into a seat across from his two best friends at a table near the back of the cafeteria. His tray was laden with food: the fish and chips special, a large chocolate milk, an apple, and a large chocolate chip cookie. Snake was always hungry. He ate and ate, but he never gained an ounce.

"I'm serious," Joey continued. "We've hardly seen you in the past two weeks."

"I know," Snake agreed. "And get used to it. Until basketball season ends, I'm out of commission."

"I can't believe you like that dumb sport better than playing in a band," Joey sighed, shaking his head.

"Just 'cause you're a loser at sports, doesn't mean everyone else is," Wheels kidded Joey.

"Don't worry," said Snake. "As soon as basketball season is over I will devote all my spare time to the fabulously talented Zit Remedy."

The Zit Remedy was the band they'd started up last year, just the three of them. Joey played keyboards, Wheels played bass, and Snake played guitar.

"Hi, Snake," a girl's voice said.

Snake looked up to see Melanie, a girl in grade eight. At thirteen, Melanie hadn't started to develop yet. She was skinny as a toothpick, with long, straight brown hair pulled back in a messy ponytail. She wasn't exactly drop-dead gorgeous, but Snake thought she had a great smile.

"Hi, Melanie," he said. "How's the swim team doing?"

"Great," she replied. "The team's really strong this year."

"You're so modest. Everyone knows you're the best girl they have."

He thought he could see her face turn a light shade of pink. "What're you reading?" she asked, pointing at a book he had shoved into his back pocket.

"*Catcher in the Rye.*"

"I love that book."

"Me, too," he said. "I read it last year, but I'm reading it again. For English class."

"I wish my life was as exciting as Holden Caulfield's — "

"But without all the sad stuff."

She smiled. "Exactly."

Suddenly Snake became aware that his friends were looking at him funny. Snake never talked about books with them.

"Well ... see you later," she smiled.

"See you."

"Why don't you ask her out again?" Joey asked Snake when Melanie was out of hearing distance.

"You've got a lot in common," added

Wheels. "You both like reading. You're both brainers."

"In other words, you're both *boring*."

"You're a perfect couple."

His friends laughed.

Snake rolled his eyes. "Ha, ha," he said. But inside, he cringed. Was it true? Was he boring? He knew he wasn't like Joey and Wheels. They had been friends before Snake had ever met them. They were both more outgoing than he was, and even though neither of them ever did or said anything to make him feel like it, he sometimes felt a bit like a fifth wheel.

"So? Why not ask her out again?" Joey persisted.

Snake shrugged. "We're just friends." Last year, Snake had asked Melanie out on a date, the one and only date of his whole life. It had been disastrous. When they'd finally been able to speak to each other weeks later and agreed they shouldn't date any more, it had been like a huge weight had been lifted off their shoulders. They'd been friends ever since.

Melanie was his one and only female friend. She was the only girl he felt comfortable talking to.

"Hi, guys!" another girl's voice called out to them, but this one was more melodic.

Snake froze, a French fry poised half-in, half-out of his mouth.

Tamara Hastings.

"Hi, Tamara," Joey and Wheels said as the girl passed.

Snake watched Tamara as she continued toward the exit. She had long, naturally curly brownish-blonde hair that bounced lightly against her back as she walked. Today, she was wearing a pair of jeans and a sweater. The jeans were tucked into a pair of black cowboy boots. Snake had her face etched into his memory: high cheekbones, clear white skin, dark brown eyes, and an upturned nose.

Unlike Melanie, Tamara had developed. And how. She had curves in all the right places, and her breasts actually swayed when she walked. Unlike Melanie, Tamara was drop-dead gorgeous.

Snake thought Tamara was the most beautiful girl he'd ever seen, at least in real life. The only problem was, the entire male population at Degrassi thought so, too.

"Look at Snake!" Wheels cried. "He's been stunned into silence by Tamara."

"Snake, my man," Joey said, "you've got to learn how to act like a normal human being when a girl is around. Surely saying 'hi' is not going to kill you."

"I had a mouthful of food," Snake said, throwing a fry at Joey. But he could feel his face get hot, and he knew from experience that his skin was turning a horrid shade of pink. *This* is why I don't talk to girls, he wanted to tell them. This is why I don't ask girls out. Because I *freeze*.

"You talked to Melanie no problem," Joey pointed out, his tone more gentle this time.

"That's different," Snake mumbled. "Who are you to talk, anyway? It's not like you're Mr. Experience."

"At least I've been on a *real* date."

"So? Maybe I just haven't found the right girl yet."

"How will you ever know if you can't *talk* to one?" Wheels teased.

"I talk to girls."

"Like who? Ms. Avery? Teachers don't count."

"You two are a regular comedy team," Snake retorted, stuffing the last of his fries into his mouth. Great comeback, he told himself. If only he could come up with sharp one-liners that left everyone speechless.

Wheels looked at his watch. "I've got to go. I have a study session with Raditch."

"See you later."

"See you, Romeo," Wheels laughed.

When he was gone, Joey looked at Snake. "So, what's up?" he asked.

Snake concentrated on his fish. "Not much," he said.

"I hear your brother was in town."

Snake just nodded.

"How is he?"

"Fine."

"Why'd he come home?"

"Just to visit. Tell me about the Zits. You come up with any new songs yet?"

Joey looked at him. "Come on, Snake."

"What?"

"Every time your brother visits you, you can't shut up about it. What's up?"

Snake looked up from his fish. Joey was his closest friend. He should be able to tell him everything. Maybe he would understand. But maybe he wouldn't. It wasn't worth the risk.

"Nothing's wrong," Snake smiled. "Honest."

Joey studied his friend for a moment. "Okay. Whatever you say."

Snake wolfed down the rest of his lunch. "I'm going to go shoot some baskets. We have our first game of the season this afternoon."

"Great. See you in three months," Joey teased.

Snake stood up. He looked at his friend. "Joey?"

"Yeah?"

Snake paused. "Nothing. See you around," he said as he hurried out of the cafeteria.

Chapter 3

"Control, Simpson!" Coach Singleton leaned forward until their noses were almost touching. They had just finished playing their first game, and they'd lost. Badly.

The coach stood right in front of him, and Snake could see the veins stretched taut in his neck. If only his knees would stop shaking. He looked down at his sneakers, wishing he could just collapse onto the bench behind him.

"Look at me when I'm talking to you."

Snake's head snapped back up and he looked straight into Singleton's face. He couldn't even be yelled at right today. "Sorry, sir," he mumbled.

"That was a real sloppy move you pulled. Tom was waiting right there for the ball. All you had to do was toss it over to him. You should've seen that guy coming."

Singleton started to pace the locker

room, stopping now and then in front of one of the players to yell at them. The coach was over six feet tall, black and muscular. When he yelled, people jumped.

When his dressing-down was over, Snake sank down onto the bench. You're a jerk, he told himself. The coach was right. I should've seen the guy coming. I'm lucky they didn't kick me off the team tonight.

At the other end of the room, Snake could hear Singleton tearing into another guy, Alonzo Garcia. Like Snake, this year was Alonzo's first on the team. Like Snake, he wasn't off to a very good start.

"No concentration! No drive! Did you think you could just stand around waiting for the ball to come your way?"

Snake glanced over at the two of them. Alonzo was short; definitely the shortest guy on the team. His hair was dark and wavy, and he had large, deeply set brown eyes that made him look a bit like a sad puppy. His skin was olive, and his body was wiry and thin. Snake thought he could actually see Alonzo shrink in size with every word the coach spat out, and his heart went out to him. I know what it feels like, he wanted to say.

Finally, the coach left the changeroom. Silently, everyone started to strip down and head for the showers. The mood was grim. But Snake was grateful for the silence. At least the other players had the decency not to rub salt into his wounds.

Suddenly, someone slapped him hard on the back. Too hard. "Way to go, Simpson." He looked up to see Tom Schenk, the team captain, glaring down at him, wearing nothing but a little towel wrapped around his waist.

Snake felt his body grow tense. Tom was a few inches shorter than he was, but more muscular. Snake had never seen such well-developed muscles on a fourteen-year-old guy before. Tom also had a reputation for getting into fights — and winning.

"You were prancing around out there like some kind of faggot."

He could feel his face grow hot and he knew he was blushing. Some of the other guys — especially Bob and Marco, Tom's buddies — started to laugh. "Oh, look, he's blushing," Tom continued. "Did I hit too close to home?"

"Lay off, Tom," BLT said. "Don't you know who his brother is?"

"Who?"

"Glenn Simpson. Basketball team captain two years running, and Most Valuable Player two years in a row."

"Well, maybe you should ask your brother for some pointers," Tom said, and again Bob and Marco laughed.

Snake didn't respond. He watched out of the corner of his eye as Tom dropped his towel and sauntered over to the showers, obviously proud of his body. Only when he had turned on the shower did Snake allow his body to relax.

Jerk, Snake thought. He didn't know much about Tom — they didn't have any classes together — but what he did know, he didn't like. The guy was good-looking in a California surfer way; he had longish blond hair and icy blue eyes. And he seemed to have plenty of friends. Snake had seen him often, hanging out in the halls or in the cafeteria, surrounded by a group of kids. Like a pack of wolves, he thought, and Tom was the leader.

Why anyone would choose to be Tom's friend was beyond him. The guy was mean. A bully. He was the kind of guy you didn't mess with. The kind of guy you just tried to avoid.

That, Snake knew, was going to be next to impossible now that they were both on the basketball team. He would just have to try not to draw attention to himself.

Right, he thought. As long as he played lousy, Tom was going to be paying him a lot of attention.

"You should invite your brother down to a practice next time he's in town," BLT was saying now, doing his best to cheer

Snake up. "He could give *all* of us some pointers."

"I don't think so," Snake mumbled as he started to take off his shirt.

"Why not? Your brother's kind of a celebrity around here," Luke said.

"He's not coming back for a long time. Lots of school work, you know."

"But he'll come back for Christmas."

Snake paused. He hadn't thought about Christmas. "I don't know," he answered as he peeled off his damp, smelly socks and threw them onto the floor.

"Come on, man," BLT said, swatting Snake with his towel.

"Just drop it, okay?" Snake snapped.

BLT and Luke exchanged a look, but they dropped it. Snake stood up, his face burning, already regretting yelling at them. He wrapped his large bath towel around his middle before dropping his shorts and underwear to the ground, then he shuffled off to the showers, clutching the towel close to his body.

When he got to the communal showers, he chose the one farthest away from Tom and dropped his towel at the last moment. He turned to face the stream of water, keeping his front to the wall.

Glancing over his shoulder, Snake could see Tom clearly. He faced forward, making it difficult to avoid looking at his muscular, rippling stomach — and his penis. Snake peered down at his own penis, then glanced back at Tom's, and breathed a sigh of relief. At least they were equals in one area of the body.

There weren't that many guys using the showers yet, so the water was still steaming hot. Snake twisted his body around, allowing the hard stream of water to massage first one shoulder, then the other. Whoever invented the shower was a genius, he thought.

Suddenly the gush of water changed to a sad trickle, and Snake felt the water go from hot to lukewarm to cold in only a few seconds. He turned off the taps and sighed. It was always the same thing in the changeroom. The moment you got more than two people at once taking showers, the hot water and the pressure ran out.

He rubbed the water out of his eyes and could see through the steam that all the showers were occupied now.

"Find another shower, you little fag," someone suddenly yelled.

"There are no other showers, you big jerk," came the reply.

The noise in the changeroom quickly died down. Some of the guys turned off their showers. Snake grabbed his towel and wrapped it snugly around his waist, then peered down to the other end of the room.

"Then wait for another one," Tom was growling. "I don't want you showering beside me."

"Do you think I like showering beside you?" Alonzo retorted.

Snake did a double-take. The scrawniest guy on the team was talking back to Tom Schenk. The guy must have a death wish, Snake thought. He could see Tom's expression darken, and his body go rigid. He looked like a lion ready to pounce on his prey.

Alonzo ignored him. He turned on his shower and turned away from Tom. But Snake could see that his hands were shaking.

All eyes were on Tom. A few of the guys stepped closer, preparing to pull Tom off Alonzo if he decided to attack. Instead, Tom's dark expression started to fade, and he laughed. "I'll let you off this time. But next time, find somewhere else to shower."

Snake thought he could hear a group sigh of relief. The guys knew that the last thing they needed right now was a fight between two of the players.

"I'll shower wherever I want."

Silence again. Cripes, thought Snake. Didn't Alonzo know when to quit?

"What's going on in here?" the coach's voice boomed from the door of the changeroom.

The buzz of activity returned. Snake traipsed back to his locker, avoiding Singleton's suspicious gaze. He changed slowly, and by the time he was ready to go, most of the guys had already left. He grabbed his gym bag and strode out of the changeroom.

Walking ahead of him in the hallway was Alonzo. His shoulders were hanging low as he walked toward the exit.

Snake caught up with him at the doors. "You were pretty impressive in there."

Alonzo shrugged. "I refuse to take crap like that from anyone."

"But he could have pulverized you."

"I took my chances."

They walked in silence for a moment, then Alonzo spoke. "If only I could be that impressive on the court."

Snake laughed. "I know what you mean."

"You're a good player. You just need practice."

"*Practice* is exactly what I plan on doing. I don't want a repeat of today," Snake said. "I'm going to start shooting baskets at lunch. Try to improve my skills."

"Good idea. Maybe I'll join you."

"Sure. I'll be in the gym tomorrow at twelve."

They'd reached the bike rack where Snake had locked his bike.

"See you tomorrow," Alonzo said.

"See you."

Snake watched him as he walked away. Short, scrawny, and mouthy. Snake shook his head and smiled. Either Alonzo was really brave — or really stupid.

He unlocked his bike and was about to pedal away when he saw Tom coming out the back door.

He wasn't alone. His arm was thrown casually around a beautiful girl, and that girl just happened to be Tamara Hastings. He whispered something in her ear, and she started to giggle. When she laughed, she looked even more beautiful.

Wouldn't you know it, Snake thought, his heart sinking. Why couldn't life be like the movies, with the beautiful girl falling in love with the nice guy in the end? Why was it that in real life the nice guys always seemed to finish last, and the obnoxious ones finished first?

Tom looked up and caught Snake's eye.

Oh, great, thought Snake. Please don't let him cut me up in front of Tamara.

But Tom just winked. "See ya, Simpson," he shouted.

Thank you, thank you, Snake thought. "See ya." He hopped onto his bike and started to ride away.

"Oh, and Simpson," Tom yelled after him, "next game, try not to play like such a pansy."

Snake almost fell off his bike. He gripped the handlebars to steady himself. Behind him, he could hear Tamara burst into another fit of giggles.

He didn't turn around. He just kept cycling, pretending that he hadn't heard.

But Tom knew he'd heard. If only he knew how to fight. If only he could think of a snappy comeback. If only he had the courage to just shout back at Tom without worrying about the consequences.

But he didn't. He pumped his legs as hard as he could and sped on his bicycle toward home.

Chapter 4

"Good supper, Dad," Snake said through a mouthful of meatloaf that evening. He didn't really mean it; he hated meatloaf. But the silence at the table was driving him crazy.

"Old family recipe," his dad said, managing a weak smile.

Silence.

"Sorry about your game," his mom said a few minutes later.

"Oh, well. We'll do better next time," Snake replied without sounding very convincing.

Silence again.

Usually, their family dinners were full of discussion. His parents loved to ask him about what he was studying in each class, especially in Math and English. His dad was a Math professor at the University of Toronto, and his mom was a literary agent, so it was no fluke that Math and

English were Snake's best subjects. His dad had taught Snake that Math was a language, just like English or French. And his mom was constantly bringing home books for him to read. Over ten years ago, she had quit her job at a publishing company and set up her own agency. Her office was at the back of the house, where she disappeared every morning after breakfast. She always said it was the perfect set-up; she worked long hours, but she was always home when her sons returned from school.

But today when Snake came home, the house was silent. He walked to the back of the house to her office. The door was closed, so he knocked lightly before going in.

Thinking of it now made his stomach twist into knots. Snake had only seen his mom cry once, when her father had died. Today was the second time. She heard his knock and tried to straighten herself up, but not before Snake saw the tears streaming down her face.

"Archie," she smiled, her voice cracking. "You startled me."

"Mom ... "

"How was school?"

"Fine. Look, Mom ... "

Snake wanted to talk about Glenn. But he didn't know how to start. And his mom was no help.

"I just have a few things to finish up in here, then I'll be out. Okay?"

"Okay." But Snake stayed where he was, hovering by the doorway.

"Go on, then," his mom said, still wearing a tight grin. "Go and empty the dishwasher and set the table."

Snake closed the door and wandered into the kitchen, feeling lost and confused.

Now, Snake forced another piece of meatloaf into his mouth, his eyes on his plate. How could Glenn do this to them? How could he walk in and drop a bomb and change everything?

His visit home was awful. No, worse than awful. "Awful" was how he'd felt when he his bike was stolen last year. "Awful" could even be used to describe some of his dad's cooking. Last night wasn't "awful." It was ... Snake searched for a good word ...

Catastrophic.

When Glenn told their parents his news at the kitchen table after dinner, they had much the same reaction as Snake. They just stared at Glenn, then at each other.

Finally, their dad spoke. "But this can't be true. You must be mistaken."

"It's true, Dad."

Snake snuck a look at Glenn and was startled by his appearance. He didn't look calm and confident like he usually did. He was staring at the floor, hunched over like a little old man.

The clock in the corner ticked unbearably loud. It made Snake want to cover his ears.

"I understand if you've felt the urge to experiment," his mother said, so quietly that everyone leaned closer. "You're young. University is the time to try new things." She attempted a small chuckle. "I remember when I was in university, all kinds of crazy things were going on — "

"This isn't an experiment," Glenn interrupted, a slight edge to his voice. "This is who I am."

"How can you say that?" his dad replied. "You went out with girls all through high school."

"I could hardly date boys, could I? I was terrified. Confused."

"What makes you think you're not confused now?"

"I just know. I'm finally starting to feel okay about who I am. Greg's really helping me with that. You should meet him. He's a great guy."

His dad's face was slowly turning bright red. "You will excuse me, Glenn, if I find that hard to believe."

"Dad, he didn't do this to me. *I* didn't even do this to me. It's just part of who I am."

Their mom started to cry.

"Don't cry, Mom," Glenn pleaded. "I'm happy. I just want you to accept it. Accept *me,* for who I am."

But their father shook his head. "You'll grow out of it. It's only a phase."

"No, Dad. It's not," Glenn said firmly. He leaned forward then, staring intently at both of his parents. "Remember when I was growing up? You always taught me to accept people for who they were, not to judge them because of the colour of their skin or anything. Remember?"

"But, Glenn, you're our son," his mom said. "We want the best for you. You can't be happy that way."

"Yes, I *can.*"

"You could move back home," their dad said. "Transfer to U of T. Get some counselling."

"But there's nothing *wrong* with me. I'm happy with who I am."

"Don't be ridiculous," his dad snapped, his voice rising for the first time. "How could you possibly be happy?"

"This is crazy. I feel like I'm talking to a brick wall," Glenn said, standing up suddenly and knocking over his coffee cup.

"Look what you've done!" his mother cried, jumping up to get a cloth.

For the first time, his dad seemed to notice that Snake was in the room. "Archie. Go to your room," he said sternly.

"There's nothing we're saying that he shouldn't hear," Glenn said. "He's my brother."

Their dad gazed icily at Glenn. "And he's my son, and right now I would like him to go to his room. Archie. Go. Now."

Snake had gone. From his room, even with the pillow over his head, he'd been able to hear their voices, rising, then falling, then rising again. Finally, the front door had slammed, and Snake had heard his brother's Jeep screech out of the driveway and down the road.

What had Glenn done to them? Snake had always loved his brother, but he was finding it more and more difficult to feel any love. All he could feel was hurt. Betrayal.

Snake put his fork down, most of his meatloaf still untouched, and took a deep breath.

"Mom. Dad. What happened?"

"What do you mean?" his dad asked.

Snake rolled his eyes. "You know what I mean."

He saw his dad throw his mom a look. "We talked with your brother for a long time. We tried to talk sense to him, but he wouldn't listen."

"When's he coming back?"

Again, his mother and father exchanged looks. "Well," his dad said, "that's up to him. We've told him he's welcome if he promises to see a counsellor. We said we'd arrange it."

"And?"

His mother sighed. "And, he said he refused to see a counsellor and he'd only come home when he and his friend were welcome."

"Oh."

"We only want what's best for him," his dad continued.

"It's not that we have anything against gays," his mom said, as if she were trying to convince herself. "It's just that, well, how could *Glenn* be gay? It just doesn't make sense."

"All the girls he went out with!"

"I think he's having trouble at school. I think it's a cry for help. But he doesn't realize it yet."

His dad tried to smile. "Who knows? It might all blow over faster than any of us would have thought."

"That's right," his mom said, also trying to smile.

Snake didn't answer. Silence descended on the room again.

"Well, who's up for dessert?" his dad asked with false brightness. "I bought some *gelato* on the way home."

"No, thanks," Snake murmured. He could feel a wave of depression washing over him. "Can I be excused?" he asked, and without waiting for a reply, he left the kitchen and climbed the stairs slowly to his room.

Snake sprawled out on his bed, and for the first time in over a year, he started to cry. But this wasn't an ordinary cry. Suddenly he was sobbing. He grabbed his pillow and stuffed it over his face to muffle the sound. The only other time he'd cried like this was when his dog, Alfred, had died. Alfred had been part of his life since he was five, and when he'd died two years ago, Snake had been overwhelmed with loss and emptiness.

That's how he felt now, but even worse. Like someone had died. Like the brother he knew and loved had died.

Chapter 5

A week later Snake sat on the edge of his bed, trying to motivate himself to get dressed. He was up earlier than usual because he was meeting Alonzo at school at eight o'clock, so they could shoot baskets before classes started.

He glanced around the room. It was big. Too big for one person, he thought. Snake hadn't changed it much since his brother left last year. On the opposite wall, he had taken down Glenn's outdated basketball posters and hung up posters of his own favourite players in their place: Magic Johnson, Michael Jordan, and Larry Bird.

Below the posters was his desk. Snake loved the old wooden desk. Before he inherited it, it belonged to his brother, like almost everything in the room. On the desk stood his own Macintosh computer, one of the older models. His mother had given it to Glenn when she'd upgraded to a better one, then it got handed down to Snake. Also on the desk was a study lamp, a pen and pencil holder, a dictionary and a thesaurus (presents from his mom and dad), a small blow-up globe on a plastic stand, and a photograph of his family.

Close to his desk, and taking up more space than anything else in the room, were his bookshelves. They were filled with everything from old Hardy Boys mysteries to school textbooks to Shakespeare. He loved reading almost as much as he loved basketball. Sometimes, on Sunday mornings, his mom would finally come upstairs to wake him for brunch close to noon, only to discover him propped up in bed, reading.

"Other teenagers sleep in on Sunday mornings," she teased him, but Snake knew she loved seeing him read.

The rest of his room was standard: Two twin beds, each with its own bedside table and reading lamp; two chests of drawers; and a large walk-in closet. Only half the things were used now; one of the beds was never slept in, one of the chests of drawers was empty except for a few odds and ends Glenn stored there, and the closet was only half-full.

"Nothing's changed," Glenn laughed when he saw the room on his first day back this summer. "You can spread out if you want, Arch."

But there was something sacred about Glenn's space. Even though he'd moved out over a year ago, Snake still felt it would be wrong to spill over into Glenn's half of the room. Deep down, he'd always hoped that maybe Glenn would tire of London and decide to transfer to a Toronto university.

He knew there was little chance of that now.

He hoisted himself off the bed and stumbled, bleary-eyed, over to his bureau to get a clean pair of underwear. He put them on, then grabbed a pair of jeans he'd discarded on the floor the night before. As he pulled them on, his eyes fell on the top drawer of his brother's dresser. He buttoned up his jeans and yanked the drawer open.

Inside were the few things of Glenn's that hadn't moved with him or been stored in the basement: A frisbee; his old high school sweatshirt; a letter. Although he knew he shouldn't, Snake had read the letter more than once. He opened it now.

Glenn,
Thanks for last night. Talking with you really helped me figure some things out, and I hope I did the same for you. You're a wonderful guy, not

to mention a great kisser! Let's get together soon.
 Love,
 P.

Snake put the letter back into the drawer, his mouth suddenly dry. He'd always assumed it was written by a girl. Now, he wasn't so sure.

He tried to wipe the thought from his mind as he searched for his deodorant and a clean shirt, telling himself that there was no point in showering since he'd have to shower after shooting baskets, anyway.

But the thoughts refused to budge. The same questions kept repeating themselves over and over in his brain: When? Why? *How?*

When did Glenn decide he was gay? *Why* did he decide this? Was it even a decision? Or did it just happen? But most of all, *how* did it happen? Snake thought he knew his brother inside-out. Never in a million years would he have guessed that he was gay.

He supposed there must have been clues. But if he hadn't been looking for them, why would he have picked up on them?

Last night he'd woken with a start in the early hours of the morning, his heart and mind racing. Of course, he told himself as a smile crept slowly across his face. It *was* a phase. His mother was on the right track. Glenn couldn't be gay. He'd had tons of girlfriends. He didn't lisp, or wear pink, or make effeminate gestures. He was so *straight*.

But when he woke again two hours later, he was depressed and miserable. Of course it's true, he told himself. Glenn is too smart, too sure of himself, to make something like this up.

His brother was a homosexual. A gay. A queer. A fag. To Snake, the words sounded ugly and insulting. Kids at school used those words to hurt.

He'd heard awful stories about homosexuals. Like all they thought about was sex. Like they were all perverts. His brother wasn't like that. Or was he? Glenn had kept so much hidden from him over the years, it was impossible to know the truth.

It gave him a headache to think about it.

Last night, while his parents were at a movie, Snake snuck into his dad's study and scanned the books that filled shelf after shelf, hoping to find some answers. But there were no books about homosexuality. Why would there be? As a last resort, he pulled out the big dictionary on the bottom shelf and looked under *H*.

"Homosexual: A person who is sexually attracted to those of the same sex."

That was it. Nothing else. No clues to help him understand it better. As he scanned the page, his eyes had rested on another word a few lines above "homosexual."

"Homophobia: Fear of homosexuality."

Did that mean he had homophobia? Snake had flipped to *P* in the dictionary.

"Phobia: An irrational and morbid fear or hatred."

He guessed he had a fear of homosexuality. But was it irrational? Morbid? As for hatred ... he didn't hate Glenn.

Did he?

And what was he really afraid of?

"You're thinking about Glenn, aren't you?"

The voice made Snake jump. He slammed Glenn's drawer shut and turned around to see his mother watching him from the doorway.

"I think about him, too. A lot," she continued.

Snake swallowed. He tucked in his shirt and picked up his gym bag. "I've got to run," he mumbled. "I'm meeting someone."

"What about breakfast?" she asked.

"I'm late. I'll buy something at school," he said as he pushed past her and down the stairs.

"Snake?" she called after him, her voice full of concern.

But Snake didn't answer. He dashed out of the house, slamming the door behind him.

"Earth to Snake. Earth to Snake."

Snake snapped back to reality. "Sorry," he said to Alonzo, tossing him the ball that he'd been clutching for a few seconds too long, lost in his own thoughts.

It was the third time in a week that he and Alonzo had got together to shoot baskets, and already they could notice an improvement. At last night's practice, the coach had, in his own way, paid them a compliment.

"You two are playing a heck of a lot better than you were the other night," he'd said.

Snake had to admit, he was starting to look forward to their one-on-one practices. Alonzo was smart. Funny. Easy to talk to.

"What's up?" Alonzo asked him now. "You've been awfully quiet."

"Nothing."

"Is it something I said?"

Snake didn't respond.

"Is it my deodorant?"

Snake couldn't help it. He laughed. "I didn't sleep well, that's all."

"Girl trouble?"

"I wish."

"Home trouble?"

"Sort of."

"Parents?"

Snake grabbed the ball out of Alonzo's hands and tossed it into the basket. "That's what happens when you don't concentrate," he said.

Alonzo retrieved the ball and started to dribble it down the court. "Parents?" he said over his shoulder.

"No."

"Brother? Sister?"

"Yes."

"Ah, hah."

"Ah, hah?"

Alonzo turned around and dribbled toward Snake, stopping in front of him. "It's just funny. My older brother Mario is causing the family a lot of grief right now."

Snake felt butterflies in his stomach. Could someone else be going through the same thing? "Why?"

"We're Catholic, right? And he just married a Jewish girl. The family freaked. Most of them wouldn't go to the wedding."

"Oh." Snake felt disappointed. It wasn't the same kind of thing at all. "What's the big deal, her being Jewish?"

"Catholics are supposed to marry Catholics," Alonzo shrugged. "At least that's what my parents think. I don't know why."

"Seems kind of dumb."

"Try telling that to my parents. I went to his wedding, anyway. I met Sari, that's his wife, and I really like her. It was a great wedding. But when my parents found out I went, they almost killed me."

"What a drag."

"Now, if I want to see my brother, I have to lie to them. I asked them, doesn't it also say in our religion to love people no matter what? I mean — he's *family*."

"But sometimes people do things you can't forgive."

Alonzo looked at Snake. "Like what?"

The warning bell rang. Saved by the bell, thought Snake. "I've got to run," he said, heading toward the changeroom.

Suddenly Alonzo grabbed his arm. His grip was surprisingly firm.

Snake turned and looked at him. Alonzo's eyes were so dark, they almost looked black. He looked down at Alonzo's strong hand, which had relaxed its grip but still held his arm.

All of a sudden Snake felt unsettled. Dizzy. He'd felt this way before, but he couldn't remember where.

"If you ever need to talk … " Alonzo said.

Snake just nodded.

Alonzo dropped his arm. "See you tomorrow?"

"See you tomorrow."

Chapter 6

"All right! We did it!"

The changeroom buzzed with excitement. They'd just won their second game in a row. Guys walked past Snake and slapped him on the back and the bum. He felt good. He felt like he could fly. His heart was pounding and he felt lightheaded, because he knew he'd played well tonight.

When Coach Singleton entered the changeroom, the chatter died. They knew what was coming.

"I'm proud of you," he started, his tone grave, "but I don't want this going to your heads. Frankly, I think it was pure luck that we won this game. It definitely wasn't skill, which is what we're aiming for. That team was the lousiest one in the league. Remember that."

The guys shuffled their feet and looked down at the floor. Snake sighed. He knew the coach was right, but he wished the mood could have lasted a while longer.

"There were some strong players out there tonight, though. Tom, good work."

From his place on the bench, Tom grinned a self-satisfied and, in Snake's mind, conceited smile.

"But you have got to stop racking up so many fouls," the coach continued, and Snake felt pleased to see Tom's smile fade. "You play too rough, Schenk. One of these days you're going to find yourself kicked out of the game because of it. BLT, strong playing as usual. And Snake Simpson —"

Snake's head snapped up and he looked at the coach, startled. Not another dressing-down, he begged silently. He thought he'd played pretty well tonight.

"You've improved tremendously. Keep up the good work."

Snake's mouth dropped open. His heart was pounding so fast, it hurt. Oh, wow, oh, wow, oh, wow.

When Coach Singleton left the changeroom, the guys swung into action again, talking, laughing, and heading for the showers. Snake just sat where he was, the coach's words running through his head. "You've improved tremendously."

Wow. This was *news.*

Suddenly, his heart slowed and sank. The one person who he'd like to tell most of all, the one who'd appreciate it most, was incommunicado.

Slowly, Snake started to peel off his clothes. Oh, Glenn. I miss you so much. At least, I miss the old you. Why'd you have to go screw everything up?

It had been three weeks since his visit home, and they hadn't heard a word from him. Clearly, Snake thought, he wasn't going to come around to seeing mom and dad's point of view. By now, if things had gone the way he'd planned, Glenn would be living with the Creep. He hadn't even called to give them his new number. If he really wanted to talk to Glenn, he knew he could track it down ... But he wasn't ready to talk to Glenn yet. Maybe he never would be.

A hand squeezed his shoulder. "Congratulations. You deserve it."

Snake smiled up at Alonzo, who had his towel wrapped around his waist. "Thanks. You played well tonight, too."

"Yeah, yeah. But not well enough to get singled out by the coach."

"Give it time."

But Alonzo didn't seem to hear. He was looking behind Snake, his smile fading. Snake turned to see what he was looking at, just in time to see Tom sit down on the bench beside him. Tom slapped him on the back, again too hard.

"Way to go, Simpson."

Snake knew Tom was a jerk. But he was also the team captain. And he couldn't help feeling good about Tom's compliment. "Thanks. You were good, too."

He grinned. "I know. I'm team captain, right? I've got to be good."

Alonzo rolled his eyes. "See you, Snake. I'm going to have a shower."

As Alonzo started to walk away, Tom yelled, "Watch out, guys. Alonzo's having a shower. If you drop your soap, don't bend over!"

Tom's friends, Marco and Bob, laughed. A few of the other guys snickered.

Alonzo stopped dead in his tracks and turned around. "I'm impressed, Tom. Stringing together a whole sentence!"

Tom's face darkened. "You should watch your mouth, faggot."

"Maybe you should listen to your own advice, pig-face."

At this, some of the guys started to laugh, and even Snake had to fight back a smirk. Tom's face hardened into a furious glare. Snake knew his type: He loved dishing it out, but he didn't like getting any in return. And he hated being laughed at.

Alonzo started to shower, and the rest of the guys went back to their business. Snake waited until Tom turned around and strode over to his own locker, the hardened look of anger still embedded on his face, before he darted off to shower beside Alonzo.

"That was gutsy," Snake said in a lowered voice.

Alonzo just shrugged.

"You should be careful. The guy's got a rep for fighting."

"He wouldn't dare try anything here. The coach would throw him off the team, and he knows it."

Snake started to laugh. "I *wish* I had a sharp tongue like yours."

Alonzo smiled. "Practice, Snake. It's all practice. Just like basketball."

When Snake was done showering, he hurried into his clothes and left the changeroom. It was a week night, and he had lots of homework to do.

"Hi, Snake," a girl's voice called to him in the hallway.

Snake turned around. "Hi, Melanie," he said, surprised. "What are you doing here?"

"I watched your game."

"You did?"

"Not just me," she said quickly. "I was with some friends."

"Oh. Well, thanks for coming out."

"You, uh ... going home?"

"Uh, huh."

"Because, see, my friends all live in the

other direction," she blurted out in one breath, "so I thought I'd just wait for you to see if you were going home, then maybe I could ... "

Her sentence trailed off, and she looked at the floor.

"Walk home with me?"

She nodded without looking up.

"Sure. Of course."

She lifted her head and broke into a grin, and Snake found himself thinking, she *does* have a great smile.

"I finished *Catcher in the Rye* last week," Melanie said as they neared her house. "Now I'm reading *The Diviners* by Margaret Laurence."

It was a beautiful evening, biting-cold but clear. Millions of stars lit up the sky.

"I haven't read that one. I think *The Stone Angel* is on our reading list, though."

"I just got *The Diviners* out of the library near my house. You know why it's not on the reading list?"

"Why?"

"'Cause it's sort of *risqué*," Melanie giggled, her eyes widening. "There are *sexy bits*."

Snake laughed. "Tell me when you're done. Maybe I'll take it out."

They stopped outside Melanie's townhouse, a slightly run-down, narrow building where she lived with her mom.

"Well. Here we are," she said, rocking back and forth on her heels.

"Yep."

"Thanks for walking me home."

"No problem."

Snake noticed that she was looking at him intently with her big brown eyes, and suddenly he felt uneasy. Why was she looking at him that way? Did he have some food caught between his teeth? Or, worse, a booger in his nose? He reached up and tried to rub his hand across his nose nonchalantly.

"I guess I should go," he said quickly, knowing that his face would go beet-red if he stood there a moment longer. "See you at school tomorrow."

Snake hurried down the street, glancing over his shoulder at Melanie one last time.

She was still standing on the sidewalk, watching him.

When he got home, he ran up the stairs two at a time to the bathroom and studied his face in the mirror. Hmm. No food between the teeth. No booger. Nothing out of the ordinary. Why had she been staring at him? he wondered, quickly concluding that it was just another girl-mystery that he would never understand.

Chapter 7

"The coach seems to think I'm playing a lot better," Snake told his parents the next morning over breakfast.

"That's great, son," his dad said, looking up from his paper.

"You guys going to come to my next evening game?" Snake asked between mouthfuls of Cheerios. "It's next week."

"We wouldn't miss it for the world," said his mom as she joined them at the table with a cup of coffee.

"Is that your breakfast?" Snake asked, pointing at the mug with his spoon.

"I'm not very hungry. I'll eat later," she smiled.

"You should eat something," his dad said, looking up from the paper again.

"Maybe later," she replied, and Snake could see that her smile was now on her lips only.

"Just a piece of toast, or —"

"I'm not hungry, Reggie," she snapped.

Snake's dad looked at his wife for a moment, his eyes full of sadness. But he didn't say anything. He went back to his paper.

Oh man, thought Snake as he lowered his head and tried to concentrate on his cereal. Their family was like an old TV these days. Sometimes the picture was clear, but all it took was one wrong move from someone and the whole thing went on the blink.

Well, he thought, we all know whose fault that is. And he isn't even here to witness the pain he's caused.

He wished he could just wipe Glenn from his thoughts completely. But memories from the past kept flooding back at the worst moments: on the court, when he was trying to sleep, or when he was in class. Last night he'd been trying to study for a history exam in his room, but his mind drifted to a day about seven years ago, when Snake was six or seven years old and Glenn was eleven or twelve.

Glenn hadn't been as perfect as their parents thought. He and his friends were always coming up with schemes and secret missions, things that would have got him grounded if his parents had ever found out. Like the time Glenn snuck out of their bedroom at midnight to pay a visit to the cemetery with his friends, or the time he skipped school for a day one June to go fishing, "borrowing" his dad's favourite fishing rod.

Snake knew about a lot of these schemes, and he always kept quiet. But on this particular day, Snake wasn't content to keep things to himself. He wanted to go along. Glenn and his friends decided to go to the construction site of a new subdivision that was being built nearby. Snake knew that Glenn would get into serious trouble if his parents found out.

"Can I come?"

"Absolutely not."

"If you don't let me go, I'll tell Mom and Dad."

Glenn rolled his eyes. "No, you won't. You never tell."

"I will this time if you don't take me."

"Tell you what," Glenn said. "I'll buy you a bag of candy on the way home."

"Nope. I want to go with you."

"Okay, okay," Glenn finally sighed, exasperated. "If I let you go, will you *promise* not to tell, no matter what?"

"Promise."

So they went. When they arrived, Snake was disappointed. Glenn disappeared with his friends, leaving Snake with strict instructions to stay put. He hovered around the outskirts of the site, throwing rocks into a pit and asking himself why anyone would waste his time coming here to play.

That's when he heard the cries for help. For a moment, Snake hesitated — Glenn had told him not to move — but then he recognized the voice. It was Glenn's, and he was calling for him.

He hurried toward the sound. It was coming from the third concrete foundation. Peering down into the hole, Snake was able to make out his brother, huddled in a corner, his face white as a sheet.

"Get me out of here, Arch. I think I broke something," he said. He was crying.

"Where is everyone?" Snake asked, panic rising in his throat.

"They took off. Chickens." Glenn started to moan.

"Should I tell Mom and Dad?"

But Glenn didn't answer.

"Glenn? Should I tell?"

But Glenn was in too much pain to reply. It dawned on Snake then that he had to decide what to do on his own. He started to panic. I have to get Glenn out of here, he thought over and over. But I promised I wouldn't tell.

But he couldn't think of anything else to do. Running as fast as he could, he rushed home to his parents and told them what had happened. Within minutes they called an ambulance, and in a short time Glenn was whisked away to the hospital.

It turned out that Glenn had broken his ankle. Afterward, when they returned home, Glenn with a cast on his foot, his parents demanded an explanation.

"Why on earth did you go to a construction site?" they shouted. "You know they're dangerous. And what went through your head, taking Archie with you?"

Snake was grounded for two weeks; Glenn was grounded for a month.

That night, as they lay in bed, Snake whispered into the darkness. "I'm sorry."

"For what?"

"I broke my promise. By telling Mom and Dad."

"It's okay, Arch. You had no other choice. I'm *glad* you told them."

"What about my promise?"

"Sometimes it's better to break a promise than to keep it. But only sometimes."

That had probably been the only time that Snake had broken a promise to Glenn. They were loyal to each other, through thick and thin.

But this whole thing now was different. It didn't count.

"I have to get going," his dad said now, standing up and carrying his dishes to the dishwasher. "I'll be home a bit late." He ruffled Snake's hair and leaned down to kiss his wife on the forehead. He squeezed her shoulder. "I love you, Mavis," Snake heard him murmur in her ear.

His mom squeezed his hand. "Have a good day, dear."

"Bye, Dad."

"Do you want anything else?" his mom asked when his dad was gone.

"I wouldn't mind some toast. But I can do it myself." He stood up and made his way to the bread box, taking out two slices of brown bread and dropping them into the toaster.

"Did you get your homework done?" his mom asked from the table.

"Yeah," Snake replied, keeping his back turned toward her so she couldn't see his face turn pink.

It was a lie. For the first time in his life he was finding it hard to concentrate and get into his work. He would sit at his desk, start to study; then two hours later he'd realize with a start that he'd barely done a thing.

It wasn't just Glenn. It had something to *do with* Glenn, but it was more than that. It was something within himself. Something that nagged at him more and more, but he couldn't put his finger on it.

"Christmas is soon," his mom was saying now. "It's only four weeks away. Do you know what you want?"

"I hadn't given it much thought," he said. It was true. He'd forgotten all about Christmas.

"Well, let me know when you think of something," she said as he returned to the table.

Christmas. Snake had to know. And it was a lot easier to ask now, when it was just him and his mom.

"What about Glenn?"

His mom looked up from her coffee, clearly startled.

"Will he be coming home for Christmas?"

Slowly, she shook her head. "I don't think so."

Even though he knew deep down this would be the answer, he still felt winded. Glenn, not home for Christmas?

His mom reached out her hand and held his for a moment. They didn't say anything. "It's hard," she said finally. "I know."

He gave her hand a squeeze, then it was time to go to school.

"Have you studied for the history test?" Alonzo asked him over the hiss of the water in the changeroom.

"Not as much as I should have," Snake admitted.

His muscles ached. These almost-daily

practices with Alonzo at lunch, on top of their regular practices, were taking their toll. But at the same time, thought Snake, the payoff was sweet. The coach trusted him more, and Tom had almost stopped making fun of him.

Alonzo was a different story. Tom bugged him every time he saw him. But Alonzo always had a good comeback.

"Mmm," Snake sighed. Since it was just the two of them in the changeroom, the water was still hot and it felt soothing on his aching muscles.

"Do you see the soap?" Alonzo asked.

Snake glanced over at him. Alonzo's eyes were closed because shampoo was streaming down from his head toward his eyes.

Snake bent down to look for the soap. At the same moment, Alonzo also bent down. He reached out blindly, and his hand brushed across Snake's thigh.

Snake jumped. He stood up abruptly.

"Snake?" Alonzo asked from his crouching position. "You find it?"

But Snake didn't answer. He felt dizzy and shaken, like he had that day in the gym. But this time he knew where he'd felt the sensation before. He'd felt it sitting in the movie theatre with Melanie last year. She had brushed her leg against his, and for a moment he'd felt dizzy and achy.

He'd felt it in bed at night, when he'd dreamed about girls like Tamara slowly undressing in front of him. He'd felt it when he'd rubbed himself in the dark. It was a sexual feeling.

"It's okay. I found it," Alonzo said, standing up, his eyes still closed.

Suddenly Snake became aware of another feeling. He glanced down to see his penis sticking straight out in front of him. Oh, God, Oh, God. He rinsed the rest of the soap off himself as quickly as possible then shut off the water.

"Finished already?" Alonzo asked, his eyes finally open.

"Uh, huh," Snake said, keeping his back to Alonzo as he grabbed his towel and wrapped it around his middle.

He hurried back to his pile of clothes and changed as quickly as possible. As he was pulling on his sneakers, Alonzo approached and stood in front of him, stark naked.

"Anything wrong?"

"No, no," Snake said too quickly. "I just — think I should go study for this history test. Do some last-minute cramming."

Alonzo seemed to buy it. "Good idea."

Snake jumped up without tying his sneakers and rushed out of the changeroom.

That night he lay in bed, unable to sleep, thinking about it.

Glenn had seemed like such a normal, happy, well-adjusted kid, and look what happened to him. Snake, on the other hand, didn't feel normal, happy, or well adjusted. The more he thought about it, the more he felt he'd always been different. He'd liked playing with girls better than boys when he was growing up. His mother was right when she called him "The Sensitive One." He was fourteen, hadn't even really kissed a girl, and was totally terrified of them ...

It seemed to him, when he looked at it like that, that the odds were stacked against him way more than they were ever stacked against Glenn.

Did that mean he was gay, too?

Chapter 8

One in ten. The figure ran through his head over and over again. At least one in ten. He'd read it somewhere, or heard it on TV. "At least one in ten youths are gay." Was he part of that ten per cent? If he was, what did it mean? He couldn't ask anyone. It wasn't the kind of thing you talked about.

Nobody talked about it in school, not the teachers, not anyone. They talked about everything else: Sex, sexual and physical abuse, date rape, sexually transmitted diseases, AIDS ... but even with AIDS they hardly mentioned homosexuality, except in passing. "It's not just a gay disease," they would say. "It can happen to heterosexual people, too."

As if the gay people with the disease didn't count. And in a way, it was true, at least for Snake and his friends. The teachers said that to get them to listen, because if they thought it was only a gay disease, they just wouldn't care.

"Those fags deserve to die anyway," Snake remembered hearing a guy mumble in the class. He also remembered smirking at the comment. But his brother was one of those "fags." And maybe he was, too.

Was it hereditary? Genetic? But there was nobody to talk to. Nobody to answer his questions.

Of course, there was one person. But Snake couldn't talk to him. For one thing, his parents would kill him. And when Snake thought about Glenn and his new world, he saw blurry, dark, frightening images of men together, embracing, touching, and more.

No, he thought. He couldn't talk to Glenn.

Snake rolled over onto his side again and looked at the alarm clock. Four a.m. At least he'd be able to get up in a few hours.

He stared into the darkness. He felt like he was going crazy, storing all his worries and fears in his brain. He felt like he was going to explode.

But there was nobody to talk to. Because nobody talked about it. And if nobody talked about it, it had to be bad.

Didn't it?

Chapter 9

"What the hell do you think you're doing out there?" Coach Singleton spat, keeping his voice low and even so the other team couldn't overhear. As he paced back and forth, Snake almost thought he saw smoke coming out of his ears.

For once, though, Singleton wasn't yelling at him. He was yelling at Tom. Tom Schenk, team captain, star player. Tom stood with his head hung low, like a puppy who knows it's done something wrong. Even though they were losing, Snake couldn't help feeling a pang of vengeful pleasure.

It was the final quarter, and Tom had just been thrown out of the game for getting too many fouls. It was a close game tonight. Real close. The Banting Broncos were winning by one point, a point they'd got on a foul shot, thanks to Tom's accumulated fouls.

The Broncos had a reputation for being one of the best teams in their league. When they'd been warming up, Snake and some of the other guys had overheard one of the Broncos sneer, "We won't even have to *try* tonight. These guys are losers."

The guy was wrong. Maybe his insult had been the jolt they'd needed to fight. They'd been playing really well, and Snake knew that included him. He'd been playing better tonight than he ever had.

But now, it looked like they were going to lose. With only thirty seconds left in the game, the odds were against them.

"I want man-to-man coverage," the coach was saying now. "Their best player is Number 12, so I want two of you to cover him. Bryant," he said, pointing to BLT. "And ... " he paused, glaring again at Tom, who would have been his obvious next choice.

" ... Simpson."

"Me, sir?"

"No, your twin brother!" Singleton roared. "Of course you! Now get out there and do your damnedest to win this game!"

Snake followed BLT onto the court. A loud cheer arose. It was a Friday night, and they were playing at Degrassi, so the crowd was made up mostly of their friends and parents. It made him jumpy now to know that so many people he knew were watching. His parents were out there and Joey and Wheels and Melanie. But that wasn't the worst of it. Tamara Hastings was also there. Snake even knew where she was sitting — three rows down from the top.

The game resumed. Thirty, 29, 28, 27. BLT and Snake did their best to block Number 12.

Twenty, 19, 18, 17, 16. Suddenly Number 12 dodged around them and broke free. Another Bronco was zooming toward him, dribbling the ball. He stopped and threw the ball toward Number 12 —

Snake leaped in front of Number 12 and grabbed the ball. The crowd gasped. For a split second Snake just stared at the ball.

Then he started to run.

Ten, 9, 8, 7. Number 12 was on him, but Snake broke away and started to dribble, fast, furious, low, concentrating, toward the basket, keeping an eye out for someone to toss the ball to.

But there wasn't anyone.

He pushed ahead. Sounds became muted. He could hear the thunder of Bronco sneakers chasing him, could even feel someone's hot breath on his arm.

Three, 2 ... Snake leaped into the air, higher than he'd ever jumped before, and slam-dunked the ball.

For a moment, there was dead silence.

Then a cheer welled up from the crowd. They were standing up, stamping their feet on the bleachers, shouting and clapping and whistling. The sound was deafening. Suddenly, Snake was lifted off the ground by BLT, Luke, and a couple of the other guys.

"Way to go, Snake! Way to go!" they shouted.

Snake looked over his shoulder at the scoreboard: Broncos, 27, Degrassi, 28. He shook his head in disbelief.

"Simpson, I didn't think you had it in you," Coach Singleton was saying now, laughing with delight. "That was fine playing. But what I'd like to know is, where the hell were the rest of you?"

Snake looked up into the crowd and saw his parents, huge grins on their faces. Joey and Wheels gave him the thumbs up, and Melanie waved at him.

"Hit the showers, fellas," the coach said now.

The guys surrounded Snake, who was still riding high on BLT and Luke's shoulders, and they headed toward the showers. Snake glanced up into the stands again and found himself looking directly at Tamara. She smiled and waved.

Snake turned around, assuming Tom was behind him. But he wasn't. He looked back up, and again Tamara waved at him.

Snake lifted his arm and waved back. He started to laugh, and he saw that she was laughing, too.

Tamara Hastings had waved at him. Tamara Hastings knew he existed. He felt better than he had in weeks.

"You were brilliant." Alonzo grabbed Snake as he strolled back from the showers and hugged him.

Snake hugged him back, laughing. Alonzo, he wanted to say, you're a great and loyal friend. I'm sorry I ever had weird thoughts about you.

Thank God he'd kept his feelings to himself. How could he have ever thought he was gay? he wondered now as he slipped into his street clothes. His whole body had turned to jello when Tamara had smiled at him. That wouldn't have happened if he was one of *those*.

Suddenly Tom slapped him on the back so hard that he lost his balance. "Great stuff tonight," he said, a tight grin on his face. "You had luck on your side."

"It was a total fluke," Marco added, his arms crossed over his bulky chest.

"A lucky break," said Bob, standing next to Marco.

Bob and Marco looked like twins, but Snake knew they weren't related. They were both the same height, about five foot nine. They both had curly brown hair, broad shoulders, and stocky frames. They were both dressed in tight jeans and rugby shirts.

Thing One and Thing Two, Snake thought.

"Give me a break, Schenk," BLT piped up. "It had nothing to do with luck, and you know it."

Suddenly Alonzo appeared beside him. "BLT's right," he said to Tom. "It was pure skill. You're just jealous."

"Why don't you buzz off, you midget?" Tom snarled.

"Looks like you've got competition for the Most Valuable Player award," Alonzo said.

Tom snorted. "As if." But his shoulders slackened, and he shuffled off to the other end of the changeroom.

Snake wondered if there was some truth in Alonzo's words. Tom, worried about competition from *him*? It was ridiculous, of course. But Snake couldn't help smiling at the thought.

"I'll wait for you outside," he said now to Alonzo as he picked up his gym bag.

"Maybe we can go somewhere to celebrate."

"Great."

Snake stepped out of the changeroom to find a bunch of people milling in the hallway. He saw his parents.

"We're so proud of you," his dad said, embracing him.

"Congratulations," said his mom. "Do you want to go out with us for a bite to eat? Our treat."

"Actually," Snake said, "I might go out with my friends. If it's okay."

"We understand. Here," said his mom, handing him ten dollars. "Have fun."

"But be home by midnight," his dad added.

"Thanks."

His parents had just stepped outside when Joey and Wheels appeared.

"Way to go, Snake," they laughed, slapping him on the back.

Snake smiled. "Where you guys going?"

"We thought we'd head downtown and play video games, " said Joey. "Want to come?"

"Think I'll pass. The guys might want to celebrate."

Joey sighed dramatically. "Our friend, the super-jock. Oh, well. Are we still on for Sunday?"

"Sure. Maybe we could see a movie in the afternoon."

"Sounds good. I'll call you."

Joey and Wheels walked away. Snake turned around to look for some of his teammates and found himself looking straight at Melanie.

"You were great out there," she smiled.

"Thanks."

Melanie paused. Snake could see her swallow hard. "A bunch of us are going to Smiley's for burgers," she finally said. "I thought maybe you would like to come?"

Smiley's was just a five-minute walk from the school, and it was the most popular Degrassi hangout, since none of them was old enough to drive. "I think that's where the guys are going," he said. "Sounds good. I'll meet you there, okay?"

Melanie smiled. "Great! Uh, see you." She gave a little wave and walked away.

Soon a bunch of the guys came out of the changeroom. They walked outside in a pack.

"Smiley's?" someone said.

"Sounds good."

"Snake!" a girl's voice called out.

Snake turned around, expecting to see Melanie. Instead, he found himself face-to-face with Tamara Hastings.

His stomach started to churn. "Hi," he said, trying to suppress the large, goofy grin that he knew was expanding across his face.

"A few of us are going to head over to the Fire Pit," Tamara said.

Snake knew the Fire Pit. It was further away, a place where a lot of the older kids hung out once they had their licenses.

"Want to come?"

Snake looked over his shoulder to see his group of friends, including Alonzo, disappear around the side of the school.

"Uh ... "

"My brother said he'd give us a lift over there, but we'll have to take the streetcar home." Tamara pointed to an old Chevy that stood nearby, with its motor idling.

"Sounds — great," Snake said as casually as possible.

"Come on," she said, grabbing his hand and leading him toward the car.

Snake's hand felt like it was on fire. Tamara Hastings was holding his hand! As they neared the car, the tip of his shoe caught in the asphalt and he tripped, almost banging into the back door. From inside the car he could hear some kids talking loudly and laughing.

"Guys, Snake's coming, too."

Suddenly the voices stopped. Snake peered into the car and smiled, but his smile faded.

In the back seat sat Bob, Marco, and Marco's girlfriend, Denise. In the front seat, beside Tamara's brother, sat Tom.

Tom's eyes narrowed. He glared at Tamara.

Tamara just smiled back defiantly. "Let's go," she said, climbing into the front seat beside Tom.

Snake felt his stomach do a flip. I've changed my mind, he wanted to say. I don't think I'll come after all.

"Well?" Bob demanded. "You just going to stand there?"

Snake knew there was no turning back. Slowly, he opened the back door and crawled in beside Bob. Tamara's brother revved up the engine, and they roared out of the parking lot.

"You were great tonight," Tamara said, turning her head to see him better.

"Th–thanks," Snake stuttered.

Nobody else said a word. Snake saw Tom glare at Tamara, who made a point of ignoring him. He started whispering in her ear, in a very low, very angry voice.

"We've been doing pretty good so far," Snake said, his voice sounding horribly loud against the silence. "I bet we'll make it to the semi-finals at least, don't you?"

Nobody answered him.

"I think we have a good chance," Snake said weakly, answering his own question.

Finally they pulled into the restaurant parking lot and piled out of the car.

"Thanks for the ride," they shouted at Tamara's brother as he squealed away.

Tom immediately threw his arm around Tamara, squeezing her close to him. Marco did the same to Denise, and Bob sidled up beside Tom. They made a point of walking ahead of Snake.

Snake's head was spinning. Ten minutes ago he thought he'd died and gone to heaven. Now, it was like he'd been kicked hard in the gut. He sighed. He could hardly turn back. Holding his head high, he followed them into the restaurant.

It was going to be a long night.

Later that night, Snake lay in bed staring up at the ceiling.

What a night.

The guys barely spoke a word to him all evening. Tamara sat at the other end of the booth, and occasionally she'd thrown a few casual words his way, or the odd smile. But that had been it.

Why had she invited him? Was it her idea of a joke?

Then, when Denise and Tamara both went to the bathroom, Snake blurted out to Tom, "You're a lucky guy."

Right away he kicked himself, sinking a bit in his seat and waiting to see the dark look cross Tom's face. Instead, Tom smiled. A genuine, almost boyish grin. "I know. Every guy at Degrassi would love to have a girlfriend like Tamara," he continued, his smile changing from boyish to cocky.

"She's not exactly your girlfriend," Bob said.

Oops. Snake watched as Bob's face registered instant regret. The shadow crossed Tom's face.

"Watch your mouth, butt head."

Tamara and Denise reappeared at that moment, letting Bob off the hook.

But those words gave Snake a glimmer of hope. "She's not exactly your girlfriend."

On the streetcar ride home, Tamara broke away from Tom and plunked herself down beside Snake.

"So, when did you start playing basketball?"

"A couple of years ago," he mumbled.

"You're *so* tall! No wonder you're so good," she said, placing her hand casually on his shoulder as she spoke. Snake was uncomfortably aware of Tom's constant, angry gaze.

When her stop was called, Tamara gave his leg a quick squeeze, sending a surge of electricity through his body.

"See you at school on Monday," she said to everyone. Just before she hopped off the streetcar, she turned and winked at him.

Oh, wow.

But Snake caught Tom's furious stare, and it wiped the smile off his face.

For a few minutes nobody said a word. Snake tried to look casually around the streetcar, pretending to study the advertisements that hung above their heads.

Then Tom spoke. "You should come out with us again."

Snake looked at him, startled. "What?"

"A guys' night out." He grinned at Bob and Marco, who smiled back.

"Sure," Snake answered, glancing out the window and feeling relieved to see that his stop was next. "That would be nice."

"How about next Friday?"

"Uh ... Friday? Uh, I have ... " Snake racked his brain for an excuse. But none came to mind. "Sure," he said finally. "Friday's fine."

Now, as he thought about it, he wondered if there was a way out. He could tell them he had other plans, a date, a party ... But they wouldn't buy it. Besides, he told himself, in some ways he wouldn't mind getting to know Tom better. He was team captain, after all.

And he couldn't be all bad.

Chapter 10

"Oh, no, oh, no," Snake whispered to himself. He leaned against his locker, staring at the paper in his hand. It was between classes and kids rushed back and forth in front of him, but Snake barely noticed.

The large red *D* glared up at him. He knew he should have studied more for his history exam, but he hadn't expected a *D*. Their report cards were due out in a week, and Snake knew that instead of the usual *A*'s and *B*'s his card would be riddled with *C*'s and *D*'s.

"Where were you Friday night?"

Snake looked up from his test to see Melanie standing right in front of him, her hands on her hips. She didn't look like her usual easy-going self. In fact, she looked a little tense. Her eyebrows slanted down as she spoke to him.

"Huh?"

"You said you were going to meet us at

Smiley's. You never showed."

"Oh. Right. Sorry. Some of the guys went to the Fire Pit, so ... "

"So you just didn't even bother to come tell me?"

Snake looked at Melanie. He'd never seen her like this before. "I didn't know it was important."

"It wasn't *important*," she huffed. "Don't give yourself so much credit. It just would have been polite."

" ... I'm sorry. Really. It won't happen again."

"That's for sure. I won't ask you to join us again." She turned on her heels and dashed down the hall, her arms swinging fiercely.

Snake stared after her. What on earth was that all about? Maybe she'd started her period. Snake had heard that girls always had mood swings when they were on their periods.

He shrugged. He would never understand girls, he told himself as he turned back to his locker.

"Hey, buddy," Alonzo said, resting a hand on his back. "Where'd you disappear to on Friday night?"

"Look, I'm sorry I didn't tell you," Snake snapped. "I went to the Fire Pit instead, okay?"

"Whoa! I was just asking."

Snake sighed. "Sorry. I just got chewed out by Melanie, that's all." He closed his locker, and the two of them started walking to their English class together. "Actually, Tamara asked me to go to the Fire Pit."

Alonzo's eyes widened. He stopped dead in his tracks. "Tamara? *The* Tamara?"

"Ssh," Snake said, glancing around to see if anyone had heard. "It's not as hot as it sounds," he confessed. "Tom and his buddies were there, too."

Alonzo's lips pursed in distaste. "Bummer."

"Major bummer."

"Anyway, I wanted to ask you, I have two tickets to this basketball game for disabled kids. It's to raise money for charity. Want to come?"

Snake shrugged. "Sure."

"It's Friday night."

"I can't Friday."

"Plans?"

"I'm going out. With," suddenly Snake felt ridiculous, "Tom and Bob and Marco."

Alonzo stared at him. "*Why?*"

"Because they asked me?" Snake answered weakly. "Anyway, it's too late now. I said I would."

"Poor you."

"Uh, huh."

Friday night finally arrived. The rest of

the week had dragged by. Snake had felt the familiar pit in his stomach all week, but for once it wasn't from thinking about Glenn. As his evening with Tom and his friends had drawn nearer, the pit in his stomach had grown bigger.

He'd hardly seen Tamara during the week. She wasn't in any of his classes. But when he'd passed her in the halls, her face had lit up with a warm, inviting, even sexy smile. Every time he saw her, his head spun and his body felt weak and he found himself thinking, "I'm in love."

In bed at night, he dreamed about kissing her, about feeling her body, about seeing her naked. In his dreams, his hands caressed her face, her back, her breasts. Oh, those breasts! It took all his strength not to glance down at them when he saw her.

Now, Snake stood on the porch outside Tom's house. It was a large, imposing place on the most exclusive street in the neighbourhood. Somehow it wasn't what Snake had expected. He took a deep breath and rang the bell.

Tom answered the door, a beer in his hand. "Snake, my man!" he said in a loud but friendly voice. "Welcome."

Snake stepped inside.

Wow.

The house was full of antique furniture

and Persian carpets. Snake glanced at Tom, then back at the decor. The two images just didn't fit.

"We're in the den," Tom said, leading Snake down the hallway.

"Your parents home?"

"Naah. My parents are hardly ever home. They travel a lot with their jobs."

The den was less formal than the rest of the house. The furniture was more modern, and at one end of the room stood a huge, top-of-the-line home entertainment centre. Guns 'n Roses blared from the stereo.

"Hi," Snake said to Bob and Marco, who were playing a game of caps with their beers. They didn't look up from their game, but nodded in his direction.

"Beer?" Tom asked, walking over to the bar.

"Uh — sure."

Tom passed him a bottle. Snake vowed silently to drink it slowly. He wasn't used to drinking, and the last thing he needed was to embarrass himself in front of these guys.

"So," said Tom, waving his hand around the room, "not bad, eh?"

"Not bad at all," said Snake. "It's great."

"My parents bought most of this stuff 'cause they feel guilty for being away so much. Isn't that a good one? Like, what kid doesn't dream of having the house to himself most of the time?"

"Doesn't it get lonely?"

"Naah. I have my friends over a lot. And Tamara," he said, looking straight at Snake.

Snake didn't answer. He took another small sip of his beer.

"I know you like her."

"Well, I ... "

"It's okay. I understand. She's a babe. And it's not like I care, anyway. Me and Tamara, we have fun. But we're both free agents, if you get my drift. I don't like being tied down to one woman."

If only I had that problem, Snake thought.

"Want to go on a tour of the house?"

"Okay."

Tom walked him through the large, sombre rooms on the first floor. The furniture was elegant and clearly expensive. The livingroom didn't look lived in; Snake wouldn't have dared sit on any of the ornate, plush sofas or chairs.

They reached a locked door. "This is my dad's study," Tom announced. "Stay here."

He came back in a moment, carrying a key. "My dad likes to keep this room locked. He doesn't know I know where he keeps the key."

They stepped inside. The room smelled of

cigar smoke. The furniture was all made of dark wood. Mahogany? Snake didn't know. It looked like a set out of an old British movie.

Tom approached a large display of rifles on the wall. "My dad's gun collection," he said proudly.

Snake looked at the guns with distaste, but he didn't say anything.

Tom tried the lock on the case. "Damn. Locked. And I don't know where he keeps the key to this."

Thank God, Snake thought. The last thing he wanted was to be alone with Tom when he had a rifle in his hands.

"Here's all his wrestling trophies," Tom said, stopping in front of a shelf behind his father's desk. "Impressive, eh?"

"Is your dad a real sports freak?"

"Yup. That's why I'm so into sports. I wanted to follow in his footsteps, so to speak. He's a real man's man, I guess you could say," Tom said, his voice full of pride.

"Does he come out to your games?"

Tom's smile faltered. "Naah. But I don't mind. I know he's really busy. I know he'd come if he could."

They stood in awkward silence for a moment.

"Come on," Tom said. "Let's go back to the den. Who knows what Bob and Marco have got themselves into."

They found Bob and Marco still absorbed in their caps game. Tom grabbed himself another beer, and Snake became aware that Tom was staring at him.

"You know, you're not such a bad guy," he said. "For a while, I thought you were," Tom made his wrist go limp, "well, *you know*."

Snake felt like he'd had the wind punched out of him.

Tom laughed, "I mean, I never saw you with a girl. I only ever saw you with Alonzo. And I'd bet a million bucks that *he's* a homo."

"You're wrong," Snake said weakly, his legs suddenly feeling like they were made of rubber.

"Bet I'm not."

"Let's go out," Marco said from across the room, and Snake had never been so grateful for another human voice.

"Where?" asked Tom.

"I don't know. Just cruising. We can bring some beer."

Suddenly Tom's eyes narrowed and a mischievous smile crossed his face. "I know where we can go."

"Where?" asked Snake uneasily.

But Tom wouldn't answer. "Let's go," was all he said.

"I know where we're going," Bob hollered as he staggered down the street, a beer bottle in his hand.

Snake held his second beer underneath his coat, but it was just for show. He didn't want to drink any of it. He tried to swallow his growing sense of anxiety.

"Where?" he asked again, this time to Bob.

But Bob only laughed.

"Here's the place," Tom said suddenly, stopping and pointing at a purple building across the street.

"What is it?" asked Snake.

"It's a fag bar."

His anxiety welled up again as he looked at the building. "But it looks deserted."

"That's the way they want it to look. But listen."

Straining his ears, Snake could hear the dull thump of music coming from within the building.

"What are we doing here?"

Before anyone could answer, the door swung open, and two guys came out of the bar, their arms thrown casually around each other.

"Faggots!" Tom yelled. The word rang out in the quiet night.

Snake stared at Tom, his mouth agape.

"Dirty fags!" he yelled again.

The two men stood on the sidewalk,

glaring at them. "Redneck pigs!" they yelled back.

Oh, no. Snake saw the veins go taut on Tom's forehead. But before he had a chance to reply, the two men got into their car and roared off into the night. They gave Tom the finger as they passed.

"I think I should be getting home," Snake managed to say.

"Why?" Tom smirked. "Things are just getting interesting."

Just then the door swung open again, and an older man stepped out. He pulled on a pair of gloves then started to walk briskly down the street.

"Frigging queer!" Marco yelled.

The man glanced around, shoving his hands deep into his pockets. "Homo!" Tom yelled.

"Fag!" said Bob.

The man quickened his pace until he was almost running.

Tom started to laugh. "Oh, look, I've scared the poor fairy."

"Let's go," Snake said.

Tom sneered at him. "What's your problem? Why are you so quiet? Don't tell me you *like* queers?"

"No ... "

Tom studied Snake with a hard, cold stare that made him flinch. "You *do* like girls?"

The door swung open again, and another guy, younger this time, started to walk down the street alone. Snake looked at Tom out of the corner of his eye.

"Fag," he muttered quietly.

Tom laughed. "I don't think he heard you."

"Fag!" Snake yelled. "Queer!"

The man, looking quite shaken, stopped in front of a small red sports car and fumbled with his keys.

"Homo!"

"Pervert!"

Finally he unlocked his car door, hopped in, and squealed away as fast as he could.

Snake was shaking so hard he thought he might collapse in a heap on the pavement. Beside him, Tom laughed and laughed. "Man, that was great. I bet that guy pissed in his pants."

Bob and Marco were bent over double with laughter.

"I've got to go home," Snake whispered. "See you on Monday."

"Leaving so soon?" Tom said between laughs.

"Curfew. Parents," Snake said slowly, the words getting caught in his throat. His lips felt numb. His body felt numb.

"Well, see ya," Tom shrugged.

"See ya," Snake replied.

Chapter 11

That night, Snake dreamed that he was a little kid again. They were on a road trip, like the ones they used to take for a few weeks every summer. His mom and dad were in the front seat, and he and Glenn were in the back. He didn't know where they were going, and the scenery outside the car window gave nothing away.

Glenn was reading comic books, like he always used to.

Occasionally he passed his cast-offs to Snake, who picked them up eagerly and read them. Sometimes he got restless and he'd lean over and poke Glenn in the side. When their parents weren't looking, Glenn would reach over and swat Snake across the head.

By the time they got to wherever they were going, he and Glenn were both tired and grumpy. They leaped out of the car to stretch their legs.

Then Glenn started to run. They were in a field, and Glenn ran as fast as he could away from Snake and his parents. Snake chased after him. He ran as fast as his legs could take him, which wasn't very fast, but because it was a dream he decided to fly, instead.

Soon he could see Glenn. Glenn was out of breath, holding his side and laughing. He called up at Snake, who hovered above him in the air, to join him. Snake dropped back down to earth, but suddenly everything changed. He saw that Glenn was standing at the edge of a canyon. But Glenn didn't know. He was laughing and calling to Snake to come closer.

Snake tried to open his mouth to warn Glenn, but no sound came out. He tried to run toward him, but his legs felt like cement.

Glenn took a step backward.

Come on, come on. Snake willed his legs to move.

Glenn took another step backward, closer to the cliff edge.

Suddenly Snake's legs could move again. He ran to the edge of the cliff to warn his brother. But when he got there, he just looked at Glenn. Glenn smiled and said something about feeling car sick. Snake replied that he knew the feeling.

He didn't tell Glenn about the cliff.

Glenn took another step back, but there was no more land. He stepped into thin air.

For a moment he hung suspended, the way cartoon characters stayed suspended for a moment before plummeting to the ground. He looked at his younger brother, his eyes full of dismay and hurt.

Then he fell.

Snake stood on the cliff edge and watched Glenn plunge into the abyss.

Chapter 12

Everything was quiet and peaceful. The city was blanketed in at least a foot of snow. Snake couldn't remember when he'd seen so much snow in the city at Christmas time.

As he glided along on his new cross-country skis through Riverdale Park, flakes hovered in the air in front of him but didn't seem to land. He glanced around, then seeing he was alone, stuck out his tongue to catch a few.

The skis were sharp, dark blue with bright purple slashes across the front and back, with matching poles. His parents had given them to him yesterday for Christmas. He'd wanted his own skis ever since Glenn had taken him on a cross-country skiing weekend last winter. That weekend, Snake thought now, was the best present he'd ever got.

Last year, Glenn arrived home a few

days before Christmas and stayed into January. Snake relished every day: the last-minute shopping spree, the conversations in their room at night, long after they switched off the lights.

"Tell me about your courses," Snake said. "Tell me about the parties. Tell me about your girlfriends."

Glenn answered all of his questions, even the last one. But Snake remembered that his answers were vague: Tall, short, blonde, redhead, good-looking, smart ... traits that could apply to either sex.

Then on Christmas Day Glenn presented Snake with his gift: a cross-country ski weekend north of Toronto. They would spend a night at a lodge, just the two of them. A weekend away without parents! It was the best gift ever.

Glenn had his own skis, and they rented Snake a pair. The skiing was terrific, but Snake discovered that it was a lot harder than he'd thought. He had to struggle to keep up to Glenn, and when they finally made their way back to the lodge, his muscles were aching.

"Want to have a sauna?" Glenn asked.

"Sure."

They were the only people in the change-room. They stripped down and showered, then wrapped towels around their waists and entered the sauna.

Glenn took the top seat, which was a lot warmer, and Snake took the bottom. At first, it didn't feel so hot, but then Glenn poured some water from a bucket onto a small stove full of rocks. The room filled with hot steam, and Snake had trouble breathing. But he stayed put. If Glenn could handle it, so could he.

"I can't wait to get to university," Snake sighed.

"It's a great place to be, that's for sure. The courses are way better than in high school. And the parties are way, *way* better."

"Wow," Snake groaned. "Only four or five more years to go. How depressing." He tried to relax and enjoy the intense wet heat. Drops of sweat rolled one after the other from his forehead onto his lap.

"It's a lot more free, somehow," Glenn said into the clouds of steam. "People don't judge you as much at university. You can be yourself."

"But you've always been yourself."

Glenn didn't answer. Snake tried to look up at him, but the steam made it impossible to read the expression on his brother's face. His nostrils felt clogged with the hot, wet vapours.

"I can't take it any more!" he shouted in mock terror, swinging open the door and running out of the sauna.

Glenn joined him about five minutes later, and they showered and changed.

That night they had dinner in the lodge diningroom, and Glenn even ordered him a glass of wine. Then they sat in front of the fire, reading their books and playing cards until it was time to go to bed.

He didn't want the weekend to end.

This year, he couldn't wait for the holidays to be over. Christmas Day had been the pits. It was quiet without Glenn. His mom tried to hide the silence by playing Christmas carols overly loud all day long. They didn't talk about Glenn at all.

When they opened their presents, though, Snake was surprised to discover a package for him from Glenn. He looked at his parents.

"It arrived last week," his mom said, eyes downcast.

"You didn't tell me," his dad said.

"No. I didn't."

Snake took off the wrapping slowly, tentatively, as if he expected something to spring up at him.

It was a shirt. A long-sleeved white cotton dress shirt. Snake looked at the label — Roots — and knew it wasn't just any white shirt, but a pricey one. It was brushed cotton, the kind of shirt that felt soft and smooth next to the skin. Just the way Snake liked his shirts. The note attached read, *"I thought you might need something to wear on all your hot dates. Miss you lots. Your brother, Glenn."*

His parents didn't say a word. Later that day, Snake crept up to his room and threw the shirt into the back of a drawer.

Now Snake skied past the few animals that were still outside at the Riverdale farm. He'd done a loop of the park. Last year this would have exhausted him, but this year he didn't feel tired. Basketball practices and his lunch-time workouts with Alonzo had paid off in more ways than one. He felt healthier and more fit than he had in his whole life. He decided to ski around the park once more.

Again his thoughts wandered to yesterday. Just before Christmas dinner, the phone had rung.

"I'll get it," Snake said as he hurried to the phone. "Hello?"

"Archie."

Snake sucked in his breath. "Glenn."

"How are you?"

"Fine."

"I miss you. I miss you a lot."

Snake wanted to say, "I miss you, too. I miss you like crazy." But he wasn't able to. His mouth suddenly felt dry, his tongue like a lump of sawdust.

Glenn sighed. "You're still angry."

Snake didn't reply.

"Archie, who's on the phone?" Snake whirled around to see his dad there, wiping his hands on his apron.

His dad must have guessed who it was from the expression on Snake's face, because Snake didn't breathe a word. Snake watched as his dad's face twisted into a grimace. He looked like he wanted to cry and throw something all at once. He reached out his hand for the phone, and Snake handed it to him.

"Go in the other room, son," his dad said to him.

"But —"

"Go on."

So he left. From the kitchen he could hear the rise and fall of his dad's voice, then his mother's voice. Then his dad's voice got louder and louder, and Snake heard a loud bang. The phone was slammed down.

Snake was inching toward the kitchen when suddenly the door swung open and his dad stormed out, his mother at his heels. They strode down the hall, entered her office and closed the door. They didn't come out for over an hour. When they finally sat down to dinner, the turkey was overcooked, dry and tasteless.

Now Snake finished his second loop of the park. His breathing was heavy, and he was sweating under his bulky sweater and ski pants. He started to ski toward home.

Their team had played really well up to Christmas, and that included Snake. It looked like they might make it to the semifinals.

His marks were another matter.

"You have got to work harder, young man," his dad had said, his face grim as he studied Snake's report card for what felt like the fiftieth time.

"We know it hasn't been an easy few months, with your brother ..." his mother's sentence trailed off.

"But you can't think about that," his dad said sternly. "Don't let it get in the way of your school work."

Ha! Snake had wanted to say. If only it was that easy.

He was almost home. The closer he got, the slower he skied. Usually he loved the Christmas holidays because it meant he'd be able to spend time with Glenn. But this year the days had been long and dull. There was nobody to hang out with. Joey was spending Christmas in Italy this year, and Wheels was spending it with family in Woodstock. Alonzo was visiting his grandparents in Ann Arbor, Michigan.

Snake turned onto his street and glided toward his house. On the front step he could see a figure, talking to his mom. As he got closer he could see it was a girl. Just then she turned to glance down the street and caught sight of him.

"Snake!" she called out, heading toward him.

"Hi, Melanie," Snake waved with his ski pole.

He realized with a jolt that he was very glad to see her. She'd finally started speaking to him again in the week before the holidays, and Snake had felt truly relieved. He hated having anyone mad at him, especially someone as nice as Melanie.

Now she scurried toward him, almost slipping in the snow. Her cheeks were red with the cold, and her eyes were bright, and Snake thought she looked almost pretty.

"Merry Christmas," he said now.

"Same to you. How's your holiday been so far?"

"Great. Fine," he said. "Well, actually, kind of boring."

Melanie laughed. "Mine, too. Everyone's away."

"I've been renting a lot of movies."

"I've been reading a lot."

"Me, too."

Melanie paused. "I brought you something," she stammered, handing him a long cardboard tube that she'd had hidden behind her back.

Snake held onto the tube without opening it. "Gee. I mean, I didn't get you —"

"That's okay," she said quickly. "I bought this for my cousin for his birthday a month ago, and when he opened it up he said really loud that he didn't like it. So, I took it back. And I couldn't think of anyone else who might like it."

"Thanks. Should I open it?"

"Oh, no. Not in front of me."

"Do you want to come in? Have some hot chocolate?"

"I'd love to," she said, and Snake thought he saw her cheeks get even redder, "but I can't. My mom and I are going shopping. It's Boxing Day, you know. She can't miss those sales."

"Well, have fun."

"Thanks. See you around." Melanie started to trudge away, her boots squeaking in the snow.

"Maybe we could get together," Snake suddenly called after her. "For a movie or something. Before the holidays are over."

Melanie's eyes lit up. "Sure!" And then, casually, "I mean, I guess so."

"Great. I'll call you."

He watched her run off down the street, her boots kicking up snow and slush as she went.

When he'd finished putting his skis away in the garage, he went into the house and peeled off his layers of clothes. He went into the bathroom and turned on the taps for a hot bath. Back in his room, he took the tube and sat on his bed to open it.

Inside the tube was a poster. He tore open the plastic cover and unrolled the picture. It was an almost life-size picture of Isiah Thomas of the Detroit Pistons, poised above the basketball hoop with the ball in his hands, the photo taken a split second before he dunked the ball into the hoop.

Immediately, Snake rummaged through the drawers of his desk for some masking tape, which he stuck on the four corners of the poster. Then he hung it beside his poster of Magic Johnson.

What an excellent poster, he thought as he stood back to get a better look.

It was only then that he realized Melanie had lied to him. She'd never given this poster to her cousin; it had never been opened.

She'd bought it just for him.

Chapter 13

Two days later, while Snake sat propped up in his bed reading, the phone started to ring. Snake ignored it; nobody had phoned him yet over the holidays since nobody was home.

"Archie, it's for you!" his mom called up the stairs.

Snake hauled himself out of bed and walked to the phone in the hall outside his room. "Hello?"

"I never knew your real name was Archie."

It took Snake a minute to place the voice. "Tom. Hi."

"Me and some of the guys are getting together tonight at Smiley's. Want to come?"

Snake hesitated. Smiley's was at least a mile away from the purple building, so it was unlikely they'd pay another visit there. It would be nice to get out of the house. And, he told himself, Tamara might be there.

"Sure."

"See you there, then. Around seven-thirty."

"See you." Snake hung up and went back to his room. He'd only read a few more lines of his book when the phone rang again.

"Archie, it's for you again. It's a girl this time."

Snake jumped out of bed. Melanie. He'd been thinking of phoning her, but he hadn't wanted to seem pushy and had decided to wait until tomorrow.

"Hi," he said now.

"Hi, Snake," said a voice that definitely didn't belong to Melanie.

"Tamara," Snake stuttered.

"How's it going?"

"Fine. Fine. And you?"

"Great. Did you have a nice Christmas?"

"Uh, huh. You?"

"Yeah. I did."

There was a pause.

"I'm calling because my parents are going to be out of town for New Year's Eve, and my brother and I have decided to have a party. Would you like to come?"

Snake's heart was racing a mile a minute, but he tried to keep his voice calm. "New Year's ... Let's see ... I don't think I have anything else planned. So, sure, why not? Sounds like fun," he rambled.

"Great," she said and gave him her address.

"See you then," Snake said.

"I'm really glad you're coming," Tamara said before she hung up.

Snake held the receiver in his hand for a few moments longer. Wow. He couldn't wait to tell the guys about this.

"Underwear. Bikini underwear, boxer shorts, sensible underwear ... My mom always buys me twenty zillion pairs of underwear," Marco groaned as they pigged out on burgers, fries, and shakes. Tom and Bob were there, but Snake was relieved to see that BLT and Luke were also there. There would definitely be no visits to the purple building tonight.

Snake was squeezed between Bob and Luke in the booth, and BLT, Tom, and Marco faced them.

"It's like they keep forgetting that they just gave me another twenty pairs on my birthday," Marco continued.

"I always get clothes," said Bob. "Clothes that are only about ten years out of fashion."

"Why don't parents get you what you *ask* for?" sighed Luke.

Snake didn't bother mentioning his cross-country ski set.

"My parents just give me money," Tom said. "That way I can buy exactly what I want."

How impersonal, Snake thought.

"So, you guys have any plans for New Year's Eve?" Tom asked now, his eyebrows arched.

"I might just spend an evening with Michelle," said BLT. Michelle was his girlfriend.

"I want to party," said Marco.

"Me, too," Bob added, banging his fist on the table.

Tom waited impatiently for them to finish. "Well, try to control your jealousy, guys," he started when they were done, "but I'm going to a party at Tamara Hastings's place." Snake looked up from his fries and gravy.

"Wooo," the others said.

"Her parents are away. She invited me today."

"Can we crash?" asked Marco.

"Sorry, guys, but from what she said to me on the phone, I think it's going to be a very *private* party. Like: me and her." Tom waggled his eyebrows.

"No, it's not," Snake blurted.

Tom rolled his eyes as he took a large mouthful of his hamburger. "Right," he said with his mouth full. "And how would you know?"

"'Cause she invited me today, too."

Tom stopped chewing. The others fell silent.

"She — invited *you?*"

Suddenly Snake felt uneasy. "She probably invited lots of people," he said with a wave of his hand.

"Gee, Tom, real *private* party," BLT laughed.

"Yeah, you and the masses," added Luke.

"Real *intimate* —" but Bob stopped mid-tease when he saw the look on Tom's face.

"So I was wrong," Tom said quietly. "I guess that means you guys can crash. I mean, if she invited Snake, she obviously doesn't care who shows up."

The other guys laughed. But Snake caught Tom's eye, and for a moment he almost felt sorry for him. He knew that look; it had crossed his own face often enough. It was a look that said, "I've been duped." Snake looked away.

This was going to be one interesting party.

Chapter 14

Snake stood outside an expensive-looking townhouse. Loud music seeped out of the closed door and bodies floated past the windows, silhouetted by the dim lighting inside. He took a deep breath, walked up to the front door, and rang the bell.

Nobody answered. Snake tried the door, but it was locked. He rang again, two times in a row, but nobody came. A wave of panic washed over him. What if this was a set-up? What if Tamara didn't want him to be here at all, and she'd just helped Tom play a nasty practical joke at his expense?

Just then the door swung open, and Snake stood face-to-face with BLT.

"Hey, Snake! Come on in!" he shouted.

Snake smiled and slapped his friend on the back, feeling foolish for being so paranoid. As he entered the hall, it was like walking into a thick wall of sound and smoke. To the left, he could see into a stylish, ultra-modern livingroom where all the furniture was black, white, or chrome. A high-tech stereo system stood in the far corner, pumping out music. Kids filled the room, some gyrating to the music, others just sitting on the couches talking and eating chips. He noticed that a few of the kids had beer.

"You can put your coat upstairs in Tamara's room," BLT yelled. "Third door to your right."

Snake climbed the stairs. Ever since her phone call, he'd had Tamara Hastings on the brain twenty-four hours a day. Just last night he'd tried to imagine her room. He'd pictured muted, soft shades of rose, tasteful floral wallpaper, a thick white carpet ... prints of flowers and kittens on the walls ... and a dresser with small bottles and jars of mysterious, sweet-smelling things placed in an orderly fashion on top. Her bed, he'd imagined, was a large canopy bed, with gauzy layers of fabric hanging around it like a tent. In his vision, he could see Tamara lying on her bed, behind all the gauze, naked —

He pushed open the door and switched on the light.

Oh.

Well, it wasn't exactly what he'd imagined. The only image that fit was the carpet: A thick, white shag. He peered around. The walls were painted white, except for one, which was painted a bright red. There were no prints of flowers or kittens; instead, posters of Motley Crue, Aerosmith, and young male actors adorned the walls. On the red wall, she had created an enormous collage of female models. Faces, torsos, hair, breasts, bums, legs, and slender, taut bodies leaped out at him. Some of the faces and bodies were circled in bright blue marker with notes written beside them: "Work toward a bod like that!" one note read. Another said, "To have legs like hers!"

Her bed was just an ordinary bed, with a big red duvet on top. There *were* lots of jars and bottles of perfume and make-up on her dresser, but, seen up close, they didn't look so mysterious.

He took off his coat and threw it onto the pile on her bed. As he started to leave the room, he caught a glimpse of himself in her mirror. He'd spent a lot of time getting ready for tonight, and he'd finally settled on a long-sleeved, button-down blue shirt with jeans. If it weren't for the freckles, he thought now, you wouldn't look half-bad. He swore he didn't look quite so scrawny any more. Only a few days ago, he'd flexed his muscles in front of his mirror, and for the first time in his life, he'd thought he'd caught a glimpse of one.

When he got back downstairs, he grabbed a pop from the fridge and greeted the other people he knew. But Tamara was nowhere to be found. Slowly he pushed his way through the crowds and into the livingroom.

Then he saw her. She was over by the stereo. Even from a distance, she looked amazing in a form-fitting, spaghetti-strapped black dress that stopped far above her knees. Her long hair was piled up on top of her head. Snake almost groaned out loud. She was gorgeous.

He started to make his way through the bodies to say hello, but stopped dead in his tracks when he saw Tom, advancing much faster from the other side of the room. He watched as Tom whispered something into her ear. She threw back her head and laughed. Then she allowed herself to be led onto the dance floor by Tom, and they started to move and shake to the music.

Snake sank down onto one of the black leather couches and sighed. Oh, well, he tried to tell himself. There was nothing he could do about it. It was nice of Tamara to invite him, after all.

BLT plopped down beside him. "Tell me more about your holidays," Snake said and reached for a handful of chips from the bowl on the coffee table. He leaned back on the couch and started to talk to

BLT, determined to have a good time.

"Only a half hour to midnight!" someone shouted above the noise and the music. Michelle, BLT's girlfriend, had passed out noisemakers to everyone, and some people had started to use them early.

From where he was standing in the livingroom, Snake could see Tamara, in a corner with Tom. But she wasn't laughing any more. She looked tense and angry. He could see her fling her arms in the air and shake a finger at Tom, who also looked mad. He leaned in close to her as he spoke, but she didn't flinch. She just glared at him, tapping her foot impatiently. After a few minutes, she suddenly turned from him while he was still in mid-sentence and stormed away. Tom stood where he was, his mouth half-open. His eyes darted around the room, and Snake quickly looked away, not wanting him to know he'd been watching.

"Snake! Hi!" Snake turned around to see Tamara standing behind him. She smiled up at him, her eyes sparkling. Could this be the same girl who just moments ago had been fighting with Tom?

"Hi. Good party," he replied.

"I'm so glad you could come. Have you been here long?"

"Oh, about three hours."

"No way! I'm sorry I didn't get to talk to you before, but —" she rolled her eyes, as if somehow that would explain everything. "Anyway, here I am, and for the rest of the evening, I'm yours. Dance?" She linked her arm through his and led him onto the dance floor.

Snake's head was spinning. It was a rap tune. Snake hated dancing to fast songs. He could never get his feet to do the right things. But he wasn't about to let this opportunity pass him by. He stepped cautiously from one side to another, trying to make his arms swing a bit to the beat. Tamara, on the other hand, let her whole body go wild. She jumped up and down, and her arms swung up above her head and back down again. Every now and then she looked up and grinned what Snake could only call a sexy grin.

Snake glanced uneasily around the room, but Tom was nowhere to be seen. He felt his muscles relax and he turned his attention back to the song, concentrating on his feet.

"Countdown time!" someone shouted. The music was turned down, and the volume of the TV cranked up. Tamara stood at his side.

"Ten, nine, eight, seven," Everyone shouted out the New Year's countdown along with the crowds in Times Square in

New York City on TV.

Tamara squeezed his arm.

"Four, three, two, one! Happy New Year!"

The sound of noisemakers and people whistling and shouting filled the room.

"Happy New Year, Snake," Tamara said now and pulled at his arm. He leaned forward, and she kissed him quickly but firmly on the lips.

Oh my gosh, oh my gosh, he thought. What a way to ring in the New Year.

Someone had taken off the rap tune and replaced it with something slower.

"Let's dance," she said, grabbing his hand.

She threw her arms around his neck. Hesitantly, Snake wrapped his arms around her waist. He didn't dare hold her tight and stood about a foot away from her. But she pulled him close and rested her head on his chest. Slowly, Snake felt himself relax. He allowed himself to hold her closer. Oh, she felt good. He could feel her hair against his chin and her breasts pressed against his shirt. Her hands started to rub his back in a slow, circular motion.

Snake almost groaned aloud. He felt an ache between his legs. He breathed in the scent of her hair, which smelled fresh and flowery. He allowed his hand to move up her back to her neck.

Then the song was over. For a moment he didn't let her go, and she didn't resist. Please let the next song be a slow one, he thought to himself. But it wasn't. It was another rap tune. They stood looking at each other.

"Want to see my room?" Tamara asked him.

"I've already seen it," he said, "when I put my coat there."

"Don't you want to see it again?" she asked him pointedly.

"Oh. Uh, sure." Dope, he told himself as he followed her out of the room.

Snake hurried up the stairs after her. They entered her room, and she closed the door behind them.

She didn't turn on the overhead light, but moved to her bed and switched on the small lamp beside her bed, then sat down. Snake's body cast a long shadow on the wall as he edged toward her.

He sat down beside her on the bed. "What if someone comes in?" he said in a whisper.

"They can't. I have a lock on my door."

"Oh."

His heart was pounding, and he could feel a layer of icy, clammy sweat start to form on his skin.

This was it. This was his big moment. He was going to make out with Tamara Hastings. At the very least, he would do some serious kissing. Maybe even with tongues. And maybe, just maybe, he'd get to caress —

He swallowed hard. Why did his mouth feel so dry, like he'd just swallowed handfuls of cotton balls? Beside him, the bed squeaked as Tamara crept closer. She took his hand in hers.

Could she feel that he was shaking? Damn! When Snake heard other guys tell steamy tales about their dates, tales he was sure the girls would not want told, they always sounded so confident, so sure of themselves. But he'd never felt so *un*sure of himself in his life. His chest ached, and his body felt like jello.

"Snake?"

Snake managed to turn and look at her. She was gazing at him inquisitively.

"I, uh, I like your room," he squeaked.

Tamara didn't answer. She pushed some of the coats away and lay back on the bed.

Oh, gosh. Snake stared straight ahead, not daring to look at her. "And your choice of colours is great."

"Snake."

"Which rock band is that?" he asked, pointing to a poster on the wall.

"Snake," she said again and suddenly he felt her hand on his arm, pulling him down beside her.

He lay on his back and stared at the ceiling.

Cripes, he thought. He'd dreamed about this moment many times. In his dreams he was so smooth, so cool, expertly pulling her close and placing his lips over hers, exploring her mouth with his tongue, running his hands over her body, undoing her bra with one hand —

Tamara rolled onto her side and propped herself up on an elbow. "Is something wrong?" she asked.

"No, no."

There was another pause, then she sighed heavily.

"Maybe we should go back downstairs," she said, starting to sit up.

"No," he said suddenly, grasping her hand and pulling her back down. She smiled. Slowly he edged toward her and closed his eyes.

Then he kissed her. But he missed her lips, kissing her nose instead.

She giggled. "A little further down."

"Sorry, sorry," he whispered, opening his eyes long enough to search out her mouth.

Then he really kissed her. He started with a peck on the lips, then he kissed her for real. But instead of revelling in her lips and her mouth, his mind drifted to his right arm. It was killing him. It was trapped under her torso, slowly going numb.

He didn't dare move it. But the pain was

getting more intense. Think about something else, he told himself. And relax! His body was as stiff as a tree trunk.

With his free hand, he tried to caress her back. Then he moved around to the front and edged his hand closer toward her breasts.

"Ow!" Tamara exclaimed.

Snake yanked his hand away. "What, what?"

She giggled. "You bit my lip."

"Sorry, sorry."

He paused for a moment. She closed her eyes again, her lips poised. He kissed her again.

He wished the ache between his legs would come back. He'd waited for this moment for a long time. Whenever he'd dreamed about it, the ache had been very pronounced. Come on! he told himself. Feel something! His heart was pounding and he could feel panic rise in his throat. He started to caress her hair, but his hand got stuck in her curls.

Suddenly Tamara broke away from him and sat up. Her shoulders were shaking.

"What's wrong?" he asked. It looked like she was crying. "Is anything wrong?"

Tamara's shoulders kept shaking. Finally she opened her mouth and let out a weird sound. She *was* sobbing. Then she did it again. And Snake realized she wasn't crying; she was laughing.

"What? What's so funny?" he asked, sitting up and shaking his numb arm.

"You're so cute!" she laughed. "I mean, you're so *funny!* You've never done this before, have you?"

Snake could feel sweat running down his spine.

"It's so sweet! It's so funny!" she continued.

Snake stood up. He fumbled through the pile of coats on the bed and found his near the bottom. He pulled it out, toppling over the whole pile at the same time.

"I have to go," he said as he stumbled toward the door.

"Hey, come on. I was only teasing," she called after him.

But he didn't hear her. He ran out of her room and down the stairs. As he reached for the door handle, a voice called out, "Have fun?"

Snake whipped around to see Tom. He was standing in the foyer, arms crossed over his broad chest, an angry, hurt sneer on his face.

Snake didn't answer. He just swung open the door and stepped out into the cold winter night.

Chapter 15

That night, Snake dreamed. It was a sunny and warm spring day, and he was walking hand in hand with Tamara down the beach in the east end of Toronto. Even though it was a dream, he could feel how soft her hand was in his. He gripped her hand firmly, but not too tight, and she smiled up at him. He felt strong, sure of himself. In control. Other people looked at them and smiled as they passed, and Snake overheard an old woman say to her husband, "What a nice couple."

Then the dream changed. They were still on a beach, but it was a different beach, somewhere Snake didn't recognize. The people vanished along with the sun. It became windy and storm clouds hovered low and heavy over their heads.

Tamara leaned into him. He held her close, and they started to laugh. She pressed herself tighter and smiled up at him, and Snake felt an intense aching sensation in his groin. He knew she knew how he felt, and suddenly she reached up and pulled his head toward hers, opening her lips invitingly.

Then they were kissing. Hot and passionate kissing. It went on and on, and their breathing got heavy, and Tamara moaned softly. Finally Snake broke away to look at her, to caress her face and see her smile —

But the face staring back at him was Alonzo's.

"Don't stop," said Alonzo. "It feels great." His hand started to edge toward Snake's groin. He pulled Snake's face toward his, and they started to kiss again, and it still felt good, just as good as it had with Tamara.

He started to move his hand toward Alonzo's groin when suddenly Alonzo slapped his hand away. But when Snake looked up, Alonzo was gone, and he found himself staring right at Tom.

"Faggot," Tom spat.

"No!" Snake tried to protest. "It's not true."

"Give up, Snake. Everyone knows."

Snake started to run down the beach, away from Tom, but it was like he was running on a treadmill. He couldn't move forward no matter how hard he pushed.

Every time he turned around, there was Tom, his face only inches away, laughing and yelling, "fag, fag," over and over again until Snake finally woke up, drenched in sweat and fear.

Chapter 16

"It seems you all forgot how to play basketball over the holidays," Coach Singleton growled at them after their first practice of the New Year. "Hit the showers."

Snake shuffled toward the changeroom, past Tom, who had been gazing at him with an annoying smirk on his face whenever he'd had the chance. Snake had done his best to ignore him.

He felt tired, exhausted. Life just sucked right now. He kept thinking he had to *do* something about it. But what? He had no energy. His mind and body felt lethargic and heavy, like he was a sponge left soaking in water. He wished someone would squeeze him out, make him feel light and normal again.

The day had gone from bad to worse. His history teacher asked him to stay after class and asked if he'd been having problems at home because his marks were so bad. Then, when he was walking to his locker, he ran into Melanie. Seeing her friendly face immediately made him feel better. He smiled. "Hi, Melanie."

But she didn't smile back. She just gave him an icy look and kept right on walking.

What had he done? Was he wearing a sign that said, "Kick Me While I'm Down?" Then it hit him. He told her he'd phone her over the holidays. He said maybe they could go to a movie. He completely forgot. And he never even thanked her for her great gift, a gift she bought especially for him.

Snake looked back down the hall in time to see Melanie disappear down the stairwell. He told himself to run after her. But he just didn't have the energy. His legs felt like two slabs of concrete. He stood there in the middle of the corridor, being jostled by passing kids, feeling like a coward and a jerk.

Then, at lunch time, he spotted Tamara sitting with a group of her friends. He could have sworn he saw them look his way before they burst into a fit of giggles.

At least Joey and Wheels were still his friends, he told himself. But with basketball and studying, he hardly ever saw them.

Alonzo slid onto the bench beside him.

"Want to get together after this? Get a bite to eat?"

Snake looked at Alonzo. Man, am I glad I still have you, he wanted to say. But all he said was, "Can't. I have another history test this week and I *have* to do well."

"What about baskets at lunch tomorrow?"

Snake smiled. "Sounds good."

He slipped out of his clothes, wrapped his towel around his waist, and shuffled over to the showers. He chose his favourite shower at the far end and dropped his towel. He turned on the taps, making the water as hot as he could bear it, and stood under the stream, feeling the pressure of the water start to relax his muscles. Gradually, his whole body started to loosen up and, for the moment at least, his anxieties were washed down the drain along with the soapy water.

It didn't last.

"What are you staring at?" an angry voice said.

Snake snapped out of his trance to see that he'd been gazing at the body that stood under the next shower. Tom's body.

"Nothing," Snake mumbled, turning away.

"You were staring at my dick, weren't you?"

The noise level in the showers suddenly

dropped. A few of the guys looked their way.

"What's your problem?" Snake asked.

"What's *your* problem?" Tom echoed.

Snake shook his head. "Screw off," he mumbled.

"Oh, yeah. I bet you'd *like* to screw me," Tom shot back.

"Tom. Does it ever worry you that your brain is the size of a pea?" Alonzo piped up, his hands on his hips.

"Shut up, fag."

"Hey, Schenk," BLT said. His voice sounded casual, but his eyes were full of warning. "Lay off."

"You're just jealous cause Snake stole your girl," Luke added.

Ah, hah, thought Snake. So that's what this is all about. He wanted to tell Tom not to worry, that Tamara certainly wasn't interested in him any more, but he knew he couldn't do it here. Instead, he stood where he was, the water still running in a lukewarm stream, waiting for Tom to explode. He could see Bob and Marco standing quiet as corpses nearby, their bodies tensed, like tigers waiting to spring on their prey.

But Tom surprised all of them. He laughed.

"That's what you think," he smirked. "I happen to know Snake doesn't like girls."

Alonzo and BLT groaned. "You're getting real boring, Tom," Alonzo said, shaking his head.

"It's true," said Tom. "Tamara told me."

Snake's stomach did a flip. What was Tom talking about? He turned off the shower and grabbed his towel. Quickly, he wrapped it around his waist and traipsed back to the bench without even looking at Tom.

"You don't believe me?" Tom said loudly. "She told me. She and Snake were making out, and he blew it. He took off. He freaked out and *took off*."

Snake's stomach started to churn. He felt sick. How could Tamara do this to him? How could she tell Tom, of all people, what had happened between them? It was private. *Personal*.

"As if he'd take off," BLT snorted.

"Ask him," Tom smirked.

Snake could feel eyes upon him as he hurried into his clothes.

"He took off 'cause he couldn't handle it," Tom said.

Snake slipped into his shoes and did up his belt, racking his brain for a good comeback. But none came.

"It's none of your business what happened," he mumbled.

"See?" Tom smiled triumphantly.

Snake stood up. He could feel the eyes of

some of the guys bore into his back. Even BLT was looking at him, his eyes full of doubt.

He grabbed his stuff and dashed out of the changeroom.

Okay, Tom, he thought. You've won. You've succeeded in completely humiliating me. And you couldn't have done it without Tamara's help.

He hurried toward the exit. How could he face Tom and the other guys for the rest of the season? How could he face Tamara for the rest of the year?

"Snake, slow down!"

Snake turned around to see Alonzo. "I've got to hurry home," Snake mumbled. "I'll talk to you another time, okay?"

"You're not letting Schenk get to you, are you?"

"No, no," Snake lied. "I've just got lots of studying to do, that's all."

Alonzo looked at him, and Snake knew he didn't believe him. But all he said was, "Okay."

He reached the doors and pushed them open. The cold January air hit him like an electric shock. Behind him, Alonzo tapped on the glass of the doors. He turned around. "We still on for shooting baskets tomorrow?" he shouted, his voice sounding muffled to Snake on the other side of the glass.

"Sure."

"You sure you're okay?"

Snake nodded. He turned and shoved his hands deep into his pockets, his eyes cast downward as he began his walk toward home, feeling anything but okay.

Chapter 17

Glenn had been popular. It seemed like every Friday and Saturday night Glenn had had a party to go to, or a date, or a game. Snake would go to bed after a night of watching TV, and around midnight or later, Glenn would tiptoe into their room and undress as quietly as possible before crawling into his bed.

"Who were you out with tonight?" Snake would whisper into the dark.

"What are you doing up?"

"I don't know."

"I was out with Alison."

"Where'd you go?"

"Went to a movie. Went to Smiley's for some food. Came home."

"Oh."

Pause.

"You kiss her?"

"None of your business."

"Come on."

"Good night, Arch."

Now Snake wondered if his brother had always told his parents the truth about where he was going and who he was spending time with. Was he really always out with a girl or a group of friends? Or was he sometimes out alone with a guy? Another gay guy?

But Snake knew his brother had gone out with girls. Lots of girls. And he also knew that they weren't always just friends. He remembered a time when he was twelve and Glenn was seventeen. Their parents had left them alone for the weekend with Glenn in charge.

Friday night had been spent just the two of them, playing card games and watching TV. But on Saturday night, a girl had come over.

"Arch, this is Moira."

Snake remembered he hadn't been too thrilled when he'd seen her. He'd been hoping for another evening alone with his older brother. Moira was a blonde, good-looking girl, and when the three of them had gone to the den to watch TV, she and Glenn sat right beside each other on the couch, forcing Snake to sit in the beanbag chair.

At eleven o'clock, Glenn said, "Time for bed, kid."

"But it's only eleven!"

"Right. Your normal bedtime."

"But last night you let me stay up till midnight."

"Sorry, Arch. Tonight, you go to bed."

Snake remembered slinking angrily out of the room, and when Moira yelled "Good night" after him, he didn't respond.

About a half an hour later, he felt thirsty. He climbed out of bed and down the stairs to the kitchen, where he poured himself a glass of water. From the den, he was able to hear a movie in progress. He couldn't hear Glenn or Moira, except for an occasional giggle. Slowly he stole toward the den, then poked his head into the room.

His brother and Moira were intertwined on the couch. His brother's shirt lay on the floor beside him, and Moira's shirt was unbuttoned and half-off. Snake could see her breast. It was the first real live breast, aside from his mom's, he'd ever seen. He wasn't able to move. He just stood there, staring. They were kissing passionately and didn't notice him.

He remembered feeling angry with Glenn. He didn't know why. But on his way out of the room, he slammed the door as loud as he could before running upstairs.

His brother had dated girls, all right. He'd made out with girls. He'd probably even had sex with girls. And still, his brother was gay. And here he was, a guy who couldn't even make out with a girl without screwing it up.

What did that say about *him?*

Chapter 18

"I got you a Christmas gift," Alonzo said to Snake the next afternoon as they changed back into their school clothes after shooting baskets.

"Really? You didn't have to."

"I wanted to."

Alonzo reached into his gym bag and pulled out a small package. He handed it to Snake. Snake tore open the wrapping to find a box, which he opened.

Inside was a colourful clay statuette of a tall, goofy-looking guy holding a basketball. Painted along the bottom in bright red letters were the words "Most Valuable Player."

"Thanks," Snake smiled. "Now I have my very own MVP award."

"I think you have a good shot at the real thing this spring."

"We'll see. Tom's still the best player."

"But to win the MVP award you also

have to be liked by your teammates. Tom fails in that category."

"True enough."

They left the changeroom.

"Thanks again for the gift," Snake said, giving Alonzo a friendly slap on the shoulder.

"Oh, look, isn't that sweet? The lovebirds, sharing a tender moment."

Snake froze. He and Alonzo looked up to see Tom, Bob, and Marco hanging out in the corridor.

"Jeez," Alonzo said, exasperated. "I feel sorry for your mother. She must cry herself to sleep every night wondering why she gave birth to a pig like you."

Tom's face darkened. "Don't talk about my mother, you little fag."

Alonzo looked at Snake. "Come on. Let's get out of here. It smells bad."

"Now I know why you two spend so much time together," Tom said in a voice that was way too loud. "Pretending you both love basketball when really you love each other." Tom started to prance around the hallway, waving a limp wrist in the air. "All you want is to get into each other's pants."

Bob and Marco started to make kissing noises. Snake felt bile rise in his throat.

Up ahead, other kids were coming their way. Time to get out of here, Snake thought, quickening his pace.

"What a scumbag," Alonzo said through gritted teeth. "What a total scumbag. I hate that guy."

Beside him, Snake was silent. His mind was racing. He tried to tell himself that Tom was just paying him back for what had happened with Tamara. He'll get bored soon, he thought. Give it a couple more days and he'll drop it.

He was wrong.

Two weeks later, Tom hadn't dropped it. Every time he saw Snake and Alonzo in the same room — which was almost every day because of basketball practices — he did his "happy couple" number or his "fag" imitation.

Snake tried to ignore him. But it wasn't easy. Especially since he felt that some of the guys, even BLT and Luke, had started to treat him differently. They were more distant. Or were they? Was it just his imagination? He didn't know.

Tonight they were at Banting. They'd won the game, and they were showering and making plans for the evening.

He could see Tom under one of the showers. Snake undressed slowly, waiting for Tom to finish before he ventured over.

Alonzo sat down beside him on the bench. "Any plans for tonight? Do you want to go out somewhere?"

Snake flinched. Did Alonzo have to talk so loud? He glanced around the room, but the other guys were too absorbed in their own conversations to take any notice.

"I don't know," Snake mumbled back. "I hadn't really thought about it."

"I thought we could go to Smiley's —"

"I'll talk to you later, okay? I'm going to have a shower."

Snake walked away from Alonzo. Tom had left the showers. He found an empty one beside BLT and turned it on.

"You have any soap?" Snake asked BLT.

"Uh, yeah."

"Can I borrow it?"

Was it Snake's imagination, or did BLT hesitate?

"Sure."

When BLT passed the soap over, Snake swore he held it out at arm's length.

Then, Alonzo took the shower next to him on the other side. Are you a beggar for punishment? Snake wanted to shout. He started washing the soap off as fast as he could, but he wasn't fast enough.

"Oh, look," Tom called. "The happy couple showering side by side. I bet Snake wishes Alonzo would wash his you-know-what."

Snake closed his eyes tight and took a deep breath. He shut off his shower and changed quickly. When he was done, he grabbed his things and left the school as fast as possible.

"Snake!" Alonzo called after him, and Snake stiffened. "Do you want to go out or don't you?"

"No," he said sharply without turning around. Why was it that Alonzo's voice grated on his nerves these days? "I don't."

Alonzo caught up with him. "What's wrong with you?"

Snake turned on him. "Nothing's wrong! Just leave me alone."

He hurried down the street as fast as he could, knowing that his legs were almost twice as long as Alonzo's. When he finally looked back, Alonzo was nowhere to be seen.

Were the guys really treating him differently, or was he going crazy? He felt crazy. He felt like he'd fallen into a deep, black hole, and there was no escape. If Glenn was here, he could talk to him. But he wasn't. And even if he was, would Snake really want to talk to him? After all, wasn't he in some twisted way the cause of all this?

He didn't know. He didn't seem to know anything these days. Even his parents were worried about him. "You're too quiet, too sullen," his mom had said only yesterday.

Maybe he *was* gay. More than once he'd felt stirrings — stirrings down there — when he and Alonzo were together. What else could it mean? Sometimes he thought it would just be easier if he knew one way or the other. At least if he knew for sure, he could try to figure out what to do about it.

But even if he was gay, he knew one thing for sure. Nobody else could find out.

He remembered a cousin of his telling him one summer about a boy in his school who'd been spotted at a gay bar. He'd been in grade eleven, and for the rest of his years at high school he'd been ridiculed, beaten up, spat on.

He also remembered a story he'd read in the paper about a young guy who couldn't deal with the fact that nobody would accept his homosexuality, and he'd killed himself.

This could not happen to him. He knew Tom was a jerk most of the time. But he also knew he was dangerous. Well, you know what you have to do, he told himself now. You have to do whatever it takes to make Tom leave you alone.

Chapter 19

Over the following week, Snake avoided Alonzo. He walked into the classes they shared at the very last minute and sat as far away from him as he could. When the bell rang, he leaped to his feet and hurried from the room before Alonzo had a chance to corner him. At basketball practice, he ignored him. Sometimes, if the practice was after school, he wouldn't even shower. He just changed quickly into his street clothes and showered when he got home.

But it couldn't go on forever. On Friday after practice, Alonzo caught up with him as he walked toward home.

"Okay. What's up?" he panted, out of breath.

"What are you talking about?" Snake replied, feigning surprise.

"You know darn well what I mean. You've been avoiding me like I'm contagious or something, and I want to know why."

Snake shrugged. "I've just been real busy, that's all."

Alonzo skipped in front of Snake, blocking his path and forcing him to stop. "Do you think I'm stupid?"

"No."

"Just be honest with me, Snake."

Snake looked down at his feet.

"It's because of Tom, isn't it?"

Snake didn't reply.

Alonzo shook his head. "I can't believe you'd give a damn what that guy thinks."

Finally Snake spoke. "It's not just him," he mumbled. "It's what everyone thinks."

"What does everyone think?"

Again Snake fell silent.

"What does everyone think?" Alonzo repeated, drawing out each word.

"That we're *queer!*" Snake blurted out, his voice no louder than a whisper. His eyes darted this way and that, but there was nobody in sight.

Alonzo snorted. "Nobody thinks that. Even Tom doesn't. He just bugs us because he thinks we're easy prey."

Snake shook his head.

"It's true. He bugs me because, even though I talk back to him, he still has the upper hand. He knows I'm not a fighter. He could beat me to a pulp if he wanted to."

Alonzo paused, then looked directly at Snake. "And he bugs you 'cause he knows it gets to you. He loves to see people squirm."

Snake sighed. "Don't you see it's not just him? Don't you notice that the other guys treat us differently?"

"No."

"Well, they do."

"They don't."

"They *do,*" Snake snapped. "And I'm sick of it."

"Why are you so worried what other people think?"

"Are you saying you *like* being called a fag?"

"I'm saying I don't let jerks like Tom get to me," he answered. "What's the big deal, anyway? What if you were gay? What if I was gay? What's wrong with that?"

Snake's eyes widened. He stared at Alonzo. "There's plenty wrong with it."

"Like what?"

"Like everything. Two guys ... "

"So what? What's wrong with *two guys?* Or two girls? Why does it upset you so much?"

Snake tried to walk around Alonzo, but Alonzo stepped in front of him again. "Would you stop being friends with someone because of the colour of his skin? Or because of his religion?"

"No," Snake said, his head starting to spin.

"What if a friend of yours told you he was gay? What if *I* was gay? Would you stop being my friend because I was gay?"

Snake stared at Alonzo.

"Would you?" Alonzo shouted.

"Are you?" Snake stammered.

"Answer my question," Alonzo demanded. "Would you stop being my friend?"

Snake looked at his feet again. Yes, he thought. I would stop being your friend. Just like I stopped being a brother to Glenn.

He didn't have to say it. When he looked back up, Alonzo was gazing at him coldly. "I can't believe it," he said, shaking his head. "I really thought you were different."

Snake couldn't answer. A lump had formed in his throat.

"You know, Snake, in some ways, you're a lot like Tom."

"What? I — " Snake sputtered.

"You're both totally insecure. You're both obsessed with your images. And you're both bigots."

"That's not true," Snake protested weakly.

But Alonzo had turned on his heels and was striding away, his arms swinging furiously and his head held high.

Snake stood where he was, watching

Alonzo's figure recede until he finally disappeared around a corner. Then he turned and headed home.

Chapter 20

"At least it's all over," said BLT a few weeks later.

"Yeah. No more seven A.M. practices," added Luke.

But the atmosphere in the changeroom was gloomy. They'd just played their last game of the season.

Snake remembered a very different atmosphere the day they'd found out they'd made it into the semi-finals. It was the first time in three years that the Degrassi team had made it that far. They'd been so hyped that day! All of them had really believed that if they played their best, they'd make it into the city finals.

But tonight, they'd played their semi-final game, and they'd lost.

"Hey, guys, what can I say? I'm proud of you. Semi-finals is no small potatoes," the coach said now, strolling past the players in the changeroom. "Thanks for being such a great team."

The guys murmured half-hearted replies.

"What would you say to a celebration? Pizzas at Mother's. My treat," the coach said.

The guys brightened. Snake managed a smile. At the other end of the changeroom he could see Alonzo, sitting slightly apart from the other guys, untying the laces of his basketball shoes.

Snake felt his heart sink. He missed Alonzo. A lot.

But he told himself he shouldn't regret his decision. Ever since he'd stopped hanging out with Alonzo, Tom had pretty much left him alone. And that was good.

Wasn't it? Then why did he feel terrible whenever he thought about it?

"Get a move on, Snake," BLT said to him now, slapping him with his towel.

Snake showered quickly then changed into his street clothes. As he left the changeroom he took a final glance back. With all the lousy stuff that had happened this year, basketball had been a constant comfort. He knew he would miss it.

When he got to the restaurant, most of the guys were already seated. He noticed Alonzo sitting at the first table and, even though BLT and Luke were at that table, he took a seat at the next table instead.

Bob and Marco sat across from him, but they didn't say a word to Snake.

Moments later someone sat down in the chair beside his. He looked up. Tom. And he wasn't alone. Tamara was with him.

Snake could feel his face get hot. He mumbled hello. He had barely spoken a word to Tamara since New Year's Eve.

"Hey, Snake," Tom said now.

Snake saw him exchange a look with Tamara, who leaned forward and said, "Hi, Snake." She smiled, but it wasn't flirtatious or sexy.

It was a smile of pity.

Great, he thought, sinking further down into his seat. She feels sorry for me. And Tom is being almost polite because I'm not a threat any more. Which means they still think I'm gay. Or at least, not exactly straight. Not exactly a *real* man.

He wished he could change their minds somehow.

Their pizzas arrived.

"None for me," Tamara said when Bob started passing slices around. "I'm on a diet."

Tom groaned. "You're always on a diet."

"It's 'cause I'm so fat," she said.

"Right. You're skinny as a rake."

"No," she replied adamantly, shaking her head, "I'm fat."

"All right. You're fat," Tom said, stuffing half a slice of pizza into his mouth all at once.

"Do you really think so?" she asked.

"Tamara!"

When they'd finished their pizza, Snake excused himself to go to the bathroom. When he came back, Tom, Tamara, Bob, and Marco were putting on their coats.

"Leaving already?"

They looked at each other and smirked.

"We thought we'd look for some action," Bob smiled.

"You can come if you want," Tom started, then stopped abruptly. "But you probably wouldn't want to." He threw knowing looks at his friends.

"Why not?"

Tom looked at him. "Remember the purple building?"

Snake looked at the grinning foursome in front of him. He took a deep breath. "What are we waiting for?" he said. "Let's go."

When they got there, it became clear that Tom had something else in mind. Instead of standing across the street, he stood right outside the door of the building.

The others joined him, Snake lagging slightly behind.

"What are we doing?" he asked, smiling uneasily.

Nobody answered.

The door swung open, and a group of guys walked out, chatting and laughing, some in couples, some single. Snake could tell Tom knew he was outnumbered, because all he did was mutter, "faggots," under his breath.

They waited. Snake stamped his feet into the thin layer of packed snow that covered the sidewalk, trying to keep his feet warm. Then the door swung open again. This time a single guy stepped outside. He wrapped his scarf more tightly around his neck and started to walk past them.

"Faggot," Tom said.

The guy looked up at him, his eyes full of disgust, but he didn't reply. He just kept walking.

But Tom jumped in front of him. "Faggot," he said again.

"Get out of my way, you loser," the guy said through clenched teeth.

"What was that?" Tom said, leaning forward so that their faces were almost touching.

"You heard me."

Tom started to rock back and forth on the balls of his feet. "I don't think that was a very nice thing to say. Apologize."

The guy stared back at him without flinching.

"I said, apologize," Tom said, the anger

rising in his voice.

"Screw you," the guy said, trying to dodge Tom.

But Tom grabbed him by his coat sleeve and threw him up against the wall.

Snake stood a few feet away, watching the scene in stunned silence. He felt like he was watching a movie. It didn't seem real.

Weren't they just supposed to yell a bit? Holler "fag" and "queer" at people for a while, then go home?

"Ooof!"

Snake glanced around, trying to figure out where the odd noise had come from.

Then he saw the guy, doubled over, clutching his stomach. Tom had punched him in the stomach.

Oh, no. This wasn't what was supposed to happen at all.

"You dumb fag," Tom hissed, grabbing the guy and hitting him in the side of the head. Then he smashed him against the wall and punched him in the jaw.

Everything seemed to happen in slow motion. Snake stood frozen to the spot, looking on as Bob and Marco grabbed the guy's kicking and thrashing arms and legs and pinned him down. Tom squatted over him and started to punch his face, once, twice, three times ...

The guy was yelling. "Stop it! Stop! Help!"

Snake could see blood running out of his mouth and nose.

Slowly he turned to find Tamara. She was standing right behind him, still as a statue, her eyes wide with repulsion and fascination.

Oh, God.

The guy wasn't yelling any more. Suddenly the door swung open, and another group of men walked out.

"Let's get out of here," Snake heard Tom yell. The four of them began running as fast as they could.

For a moment Snake stood there, still frozen. He saw the looks of horror and alarm cross the other men's faces. He saw the young guy on the ground curl into a ball, clutching his legs tightly against his chest, moaning softly.

He started to run, too. As fast as he could. But he ran in the other direction. When he saw them on Monday, he told himself, he would tell them he must have lost them when they took off.

When he got home he ran upstairs to the bathroom and closed the door. He bent over the toilet and vomited until there was nothing left and his insides felt empty and raw.

That guy has a family and friends, he thought as he slid down onto the hard tiles of the bathroom floor. He probably has a job, or goes to school. Maybe he lives with his parents. Maybe he has his own apartment. He might have a dog or a cat at home. Maybe he likes to read, or go to movies.

He looked so average, Snake thought as he sat shivering on the floor, shivering like mad even though it wasn't cold.

He could have been anybody.

He could have been Glenn.

Chapter 21

"Archie, what is wrong with you?" his mother's eyes were full of concern. They were sitting around the kitchen table, their dinner in front of them, so far untouched.

"Nothing."

"Please, son. We love you," his dad said.

Snake didn't reply. He just stared at his plate.

"You know you can talk to us."

"Like Glenn could talk to you?" he blurted out, his eyes burning.

His parents were silent. They looked at each other.

"Archie's right," his mom said quietly.

"It's a completely different situation —" his dad began.

Snake scraped back his chair. "I'm going to my room."

"Archie!" his mom cried. "Come back. Let's talk."

But Snake took the stairs two at a time and locked himself into his room.

A black cloud hung over his head. He felt overwhelmed with hate. He hated Tom. He hated Tamara, and Bob, and Marco. But most of all, he hated himself. He hadn't been the one to land the punches. But he'd done nothing to stop it. And he knew that made him just as guilty as Tom.

All because he didn't want them to think he was gay, he thought now with disgust.

He stood up and looked at himself in the mirror. "You're disgusting," he whispered to his image. He thought back to Alonzo's words: "In some ways, you're a lot like Tom."

Snake swallowed. He didn't want to be like Tom. He didn't want to be "like" anyone. He just wanted to be himself, whoever and whatever that was.

The house was dark. It was after midnight. He could hear his parents' steady breathing as he passed by their bedroom door. He tiptoed down the stairs and into the kitchen.

As quietly as possible, he picked up the phone and dialed.

"Directory assistance for what city?" the operator said.

"London, Ontario."

"Hello?" a tired voice said on the other end.

"Glenn?"

"No. Just a minute."

Snake stared into the mouth piece. Was that Greg? He thought he could hear two voices murmuring to each other on the other end of the line. Did they sleep in the same bed?

"Hello?" his brother's voice came on the line. "Who is this?"

"Glenn?"

"Arch?"

And suddenly he was crying. Sobbing. He put his hand over his mouth to muffle the sound, not wanting to wake his parents.

"Arch, what's wrong?"

Snake couldn't answer. He just kept on crying.

"Calm down. Take a deep breath. You know you can tell me what's on your mind."

"I don't know," Snake managed to say, his voice cracking. "Everything seems wrong."

"I remember that feeling," Glenn said softly. "I miss you so much, Arch. I really do."

"I miss you, too."

There was a moment of silence on the phone, except for Snake's occasional uncontrollable sob.

"I can't stand this," Glenn said, his voice

defiant. "I'm coming up. I need to see you. We need to talk. *You* need to talk."

"No!" Snake said. "I mean, Mom and Dad ..."

"It doesn't matter. It's you I'm worried about. You're my brother."

Snake's mind was racing. If Glenn came home, there would be another scene, another fight. Snake knew he couldn't handle that.

"I've got a better idea," he said. "I'll come visit you. In London."

There was another pause. "Okay. If that's what you want. I'd love it if you came here."

"Can I come soon? Like, this weekend?"

"Sure. What are you going to tell Mom and Dad?"

"I'll think of something."

"Do you have money for the train?"

"I think so."

"If you buy your ticket in Toronto, I'll pay you for it when you get here."

"I'll come on the morning train, on Saturday."

"I'll be at the station."

"Okay."

"I'm really looking forward to this, Arch."

"Me, too."

"I love you."

Snake's hand was shaking. He wiped some of the tears from his face. He said, quietly, "Me, too."

Chapter 22

The train zipped past the endless lookalike suburbs and boroughs that stretched further and further from Toronto every year. Snake stared out the window at the row upon row of identical houses and the occasional small sapling that had been planted in place of the towering old trees that had stood there before the construction had begun.

He could see his own reflection in the glass, superimposed over the bland scenery. He tried to stare deep into his own eyes, as if hoping to see an answer to a question he didn't know, but they didn't tell him anything.

You should try to sleep, he told himself, but he knew it was impossible. Ever since he'd spoken to his brother on Monday, he'd tossed and turned in bed every night, wondering if this was the right decision. More than once he'd picked up the phone to call Glenn and tell him he couldn't visit, after all. But he'd always hung up mid-dial.

By Thursday afternoon, he'd made up his mind that he was going to go. But he knew he couldn't tell his parents the truth. So he concocted a lie. But he needed some help.

After school, he waited for Joey by his locker.

"Hey, Snake!" Joey said, slapping his friend on the back. "Sorry about your last game. But you still did really well. You were one of the best players on the team."

"Thanks."

"I guess this means we can resume our friendship full-time?" he teased.

"Yeah. It does," Snake smiled. You don't know how much I've missed you, he'd wanted to say. "Listen, I need to ask you a favour."

"Shoot."

"Can we go somewhere? To Smiley's or something?"

"You buying?"

"Sure."

"Let's go."

"I need you to cover for me this weekend," Snake told him over fries and gravy.

"Why?"

"I'm going to visit my brother in London."

"So?"

"So, my parents and my brother had a falling-out a while back. I know if I asked them, they'd say no. But I really need to see him."

"What kind of falling-out?"

"It's a long story."

"I've got time."

"I'd rather not talk about it."

"Look, Snake. I'm your best friend, right?"

"Yeah."

"And you're also asking me to lie for you. If I'm going to lie for you, I have to know *why* I'm doing it."

Snake studied Joey for a moment. "You won't tell anyone?"

"Promise."

He took a deep breath. "Glenn is gay." It was surprising how easily the words slipped off his tongue. It was the first time he'd said them out loud.

Joey's mouth dropped open. "Glenn?"

Snake nodded.

"Wow."

"He told us last October."

"Wow," Joey murmured again. "Your poor brother."

"He says he's happy."

"I don't mean now. I mean, growing up. He must have felt so alone."

Snake shrugged. "I don't know. He always seemed happy to me."

"But imagine never being able to talk about it ... Why is that, anyway? Why don't people talk about it?"

"I don't know."

"I think it's good you're going to visit him," Joey had said. "He needs his family."

"So, you'll cover for me? Saturday and Sunday? I'll be home by dinner on Sunday."

"No problem. Tell them you're coming over in the morning to practice with The Zits, and that you're going to spend the night. I'll be home in the evening, anyway, so I can make sure I answer the phone."

"Thanks, Joey. I really appreciate it."

"It's no problem. I hope it's a good visit."

"Next stop, London," the conductor announced.

Snake got his gym bag down from the overhead compartment and perched on the edge of his seat, waiting for the train to slow down.

But when it stopped, he didn't move. He let all the other passengers go by, then, finally, he stepped out into the aisle and toward the doors.

When he stepped onto the platform, he didn't see Glenn at first. He wandered toward the station entrance, looking from left to right. Then he saw him. He was standing at the far end of the platform, and his eyes met Snake's at the same time. He walked quickly toward Snake.

"Archie," he said, breaking into a grin.

He put his arms around Snake, and for a moment, Snake stiffened. But only for a moment. He felt his body relax and he threw his arms around Glenn. He could feel his eyes start to sting, so he squeezed them shut and buried his face in Glenn's shoulder.

They stood like that for a long time. Snake felt like he never wanted to let go.

It was after one A.M. when Snake finally went to bed. He lay under the covers, feeling warm and happy inside. What a great day! Glenn had taken him on a tour of the university in his Jeep. Then they'd driven through downtown London to his apartment.

"Is, uh, what's-his-name going to be there?" Snake mumbled.

"Greg? No, he isn't. He decided to make himself scarce so we could visit."

Snake breathed a quiet sigh of relief.

"But you'll still get a chance to meet him," Glenn continued as they pulled into the driveway of an old building, and Snake felt his stomach sink again. "He'll be coming back late tonight or tomorrow."

When Glenn opened the door to the apartment, Snake laughed. At least in some ways, Glenn hadn't changed a bit.

"It's a pig-sty!" he said.

"I know, I know," Glenn groaned. "I was kind of hoping Greg would be the neat type, you know? But he's worse than me."

Snake felt himself stiffen. Did Glenn have to mention Greg?

"Take a tour. I'm going to make lunch," Glenn said.

The first thing Snake noticed was that there were two bedrooms. They probably didn't sleep together, after all, he told himself. Why would they have a two-bedroom apartment, with two beds and everything, if they didn't use them?

"Tuna fish sandwiches, coming up," Glenn hollered from the kitchen.

"Sounds great," Snake replied, joining him.

Glenn slid a sandwich onto the plate in front of him. "How are Mom and Dad?" he asked.

Snake paused. "Mom misses you like crazy. I can tell. I think she wants to work things out. But Dad ... "

"That's what I thought."

"I know he misses you. But you know how he is. He tries not to show it."

Glenn nodded. Snake saw the hurt in his eyes. He played with the crumbs on his plate. "It's awful there without you, Glenn. Christmas was terrible."

"Yeah, well. My Christmas wasn't so hot, either."

"Where were you?"

"At Greg's family's."

"Oh. Do they know about ... you know?"

"The fact that we're lovers?" Glenn said. "You don't have to be afraid to say it, Arch."

Snake didn't answer.

"They don't know. I wish they did, but they don't. They just thought I was a poor orphaned friend of their son's, who didn't have anywhere to go for the holidays."

Suddenly Snake felt angry with Greg. "Why doesn't Greg tell them? It's not right, lying to them like that."

Glenn stared at Snake and laughed in disbelief. "Why do *you* think? We decided in September that we were both going to tell our families. I happened to visit home first. He saw what happened to me ... being *banished* from our home ... He was terrified the same thing would happen to him. I can't blame him."

Snake's face felt like it was burning. Why was Glenn yelling at *him? He* hadn't done anything wrong.

Then Glenn cleared his throat. "I was thinking we could go shoot some baskets at the university," he said.

Snake brightened. "Great! I can show you all the stuff I've learned."

They played for almost two hours, then Glenn took him out to dinner at a favourite university hangout. Afterwards, they went to a movie, and when they got home, Glenn even let Snake have a beer. What an excellent day, he thought again. Hanging out. Just the two of them. Just like old times. It was hard to believe anything had changed. There was *something* different, though. About Glenn. Snake had been trying to put his finger on what it was all day, without success.

He couldn't wait for tomorrow. Greg hadn't come back, and Glenn said he guessed he wouldn't be coming back till some time on Sunday. By then, Snake and Glenn would be out having fun.

I made the right decision, he thought. I'm glad I came.

He was exhausted. He closed his eyes and slept like a log, better than he had in months.

He woke with a start. Sunlight was pouring in through the window. It felt late. He picked up his watch, which lay beside him on the floor. Ten o'clock! Snake hardly ever slept in that late. He jumped out of bed. His train left at three. That meant he and Glenn had less than five more hours to be together.

He stumbled into the bathroom and had

a quick shower. I'll make a big breakfast this morning, he thought as he slipped into his jeans and shirt. A feast. Bacon, eggs, toast, orange juice. He surveyed the rest of the apartment. There was no sign of life.

Snake was restless. Glenn wouldn't mind if he woke him; he was sure of it. He tiptoed over to Glenn's door and listened. Not a peep. He knocked timidly on the door, and when there was no answer, he knocked a bit louder. "Glenn?"

"That you, Arch?" a sleepy voice said.

Snake pushed open the door. "It's after ten, so I thought —"

He froze. Glenn was not alone. He had his arm thrown around another guy, who was still sleeping. They were naked, at least from the waist up. The sheets hid the rest of their bodies.

Suddenly the guy beside Glenn stirred. "Time to get up?" he mumbled.

"This," smiled Glenn, "is Greg."

Snake didn't smile back. He slammed the door as hard as he could.

His heart was racing as he paced back and forth in the livingroom. Everything was going so well. Why did that guy have to come back?

The bedroom door swung open. Snake turned around to see Glenn, his face set into a stony glare.

"What the hell was that all about?" he said in a low, angry voice.

"How do you expect me to act?" Snake said, almost shouting.

Glenn shook his head. "I expect you to act *nice*. I told you I was living with a guy. That I loved him. What did you think? That we were just good friends?"

The bedroom door opened again, and Greg poked his head out. Glenn and Snake fell silent.

"Don't let me interrupt," he said, raising his eyebrows at Glenn as he passed by. "I'm just going to have a shower."

When Greg was gone, Glenn turned again to Snake. "When he gets out, I want you to *be nice*. You're in our house now. I won't put up with any of your snide remarks. Got it?"

Snake didn't answer. He just started to shuffle toward the kitchen.

"Got it?" Glenn said again, his voice rising.

Snake turned and looked at Glenn. "Got it," he said through clenched teeth.

The three of them ate breakfast in silence. Usually Snake loved bacon and eggs, but today, they stuck in his throat. His mind was racing. He tried to size up Greg with sidelong glances as he finished the eggs. Greg didn't *look* gay. He didn't lisp or wiggle his bum when he walked. He looked so *normal*.

He was shorter than Glenn by a few inches, and his hair was red. He had a pleasant face. Snake thought he was the kind of guy that the girls around school would call "cute." He was wearing a pair of jeans and a T-shirt.

"So, Glenn tells me you're a big reader," Greg said now.

Snake shrugged. "I guess so," he muttered.

"Greg's studying Canadian literature. Getting his Masters," Glenn said, smiling at Greg.

"I haven't read many Canadian books," Snake mumbled.

"A lot of people haven't," Greg said. "They don't know what they're missing."

Snake dug into his eggs again. He knew what Greg was trying to do. He was trying to butter him up. Well, it wouldn't work. "Could you pass the salt?" he mumbled to Greg.

"Sure," said Greg, passing the shaker to Snake.

Only then did he notice Greg's T-shirt. "Gay Pride," it said in large, bold black lettering.

He choked on his mouthful of orange juice.

"I thought after breakfast we could go to

the fair grounds," Glenn was saying. "There's a big auto show down there."

Greg groaned. "You and cars. Oh, well. I dragged you to the art gallery last week, so I guess I can handle cars for one day."

"What do you say, Arch? Sound good?"

Snake could feel his face getting hotter and hotter. He couldn't tear his eyes away from Greg's T-shirt. "Do you wear it out?" Snake blurted.

Greg's eyes crinkled with laughter and he smiled. "As often as I can. I figure if I can't be out to my family, then I can at least be out here. This T-shirt makes me feel good. Proud."

"But, what will ... "

"What will people think?" Glenn finished his sentence for him. "They can think what they want. If we were black, we wouldn't try to hide the colour of our skin. If we were straight, we wouldn't try to hide it."

"I'm beyond caring what people here think," Greg added. "If someone doesn't like me because of my sexuality, then I don't want him as a friend, anyway."

"What about your family, then?" Snake challenged. "You're not open with them."

Greg paused, his fork poised near his mouth. The crinkles around his eyes disappeared and his smile faded.

"You're right. Some day, I will be." He

looked down at his plate. "I've been making it sound like it's easy. But it's not.

They fell silent. Snake watched out of the corner of his eye as Glenn reached out and squeezed Greg's hand.

"Well. I guess I should get in line." Snake and Glenn sat in the Jeep outside the train station. It was twenty to three.

What a day. When they'd gone to the auto show, Greg had taken off his coat and slung it over his arm, so the whole world could read his T-shirt. Snake had been mortified. He'd walked a few paces behind them, cringing every time someone walked by.

To his surprise, though, only a few people had glanced at one another as they'd passed. He'd seen two guys exchange whispers and looks of disgust. But that was it.

After the auto show they'd wandered along Richmond Street and through the park. At one point Glenn had actually held Greg's hand. A group of young guys nearby had yelled out, "faggots!" Glenn and Greg had just ignored them, but Snake had been flooded with emotion.

His first thought was that they were dumb to hold hands. But other images quickly flooded his brain: His first visit to the purple building; his mouth spewing out the same word these jerks had just yelled at his brother: "Fag. Homo. Queer." The young guy lying on the pavement, blood trickling out of his mouth. Tom's fist coming down on his jaw. And Snake himself, standing dead still, his eyes wide with terror, not doing a damn thing.

Now, he sat with his hand on the door handle. "It was good seeing you, Glenn."

"It was good seeing you, too."

They were silent for a moment.

"Why do you like guys?" Snake asked all of a sudden. "Why would you rather have sex with guys than girls?"

Quickly he lowered his head. He could feel Glenn's eyes on him.

"It's not just about sex," he said. "It's about who I am. Sex is just a small part of it. There's also love, feelings. Identity."

Snake fell silent.

"I love Greg. He makes me feel good about myself. Happy."

"But you were always happy," Snake said.

Glenn shook his head, but all he said was, "You'll be late for your train."

Snake opened the door and jumped out, grabbing his bag from the back seat.

"Thanks for having me," he said as he closed the door.

Glenn hopped out of the driver's seat and walked over to Snake. They hugged, but it was brief. Stiff.

Glenn climbed back into the Jeep and Snake started to walk toward the station.

"Arch?"

Snake turned around.

"I wasn't, you know."

"What?"

"Happy. I wasn't always happy."

Glenn turned the key in the ignition and drove away.

Chapter 23

Later that night he spoke with Joey, dragging the upstairs hall phone into his bedroom and closing the door.

"Your parents never phoned here," Joey said.

"All they asked me when I came in is if I'd had a good weekend," Snake replied.

"So. Did you?"

"Did I what?"

"Have a good weekend."

Snake paused. "Saturday was great. Today wasn't so great."

"How come?"

"I met *him*."

"Oh," Joey said. "Was he a jerk?"

"No."

"Was he *kind of* a jerk?"

"No."

"Was he boring?"

"No."

"Is it the way he treats your brother?"

"No, not at all." Snake sighed. "It was just the *idea,* you know?"

Joey was quiet for a moment. "I guess ..."

"You think I'm overreacting."

"I never said that."

"But you're thinking it."

"No, I'm not."

There was another pause. "It's complicated," Snake said.

"Yeah."

"I guess I should go," Snake said. "I've got lots of homework to catch up on."

"See you at school tomorrow."

"Thanks a lot, Joey. For everything."

"No problem. Any time."

Snake hung up. He put the phone back in its proper place, then quickly unpacked his overnight bag.

There was something in the side pouch. He pulled it out. It was a book called *The Tin Flute,* by Gabrielle Roy. Snake opened the cover.

"This is one of my favourite Canadian books. It's rather depressing, but beautifully written. I hope you enjoy it. Greg."

That night, Snake lay on top of his covers, still fully clothed. Glenn's words raced through his brain. "I wasn't always happy." Was it true? He let his mind wander back to when he and Glenn shared this room.

But this time, he tried to *really* remember.

He forced up memories that he had cast aside years ago and replaced with happier ones. Like when Glenn was thirteen and he was eight. Snake winced at the images that popped into his head, but he made himself continue. He remembered Glenn, crying himself to sleep while he listened to his muffled sobs in the darkness, frightened and helpless.

And it hadn't been just one night. Night after night, the same thing had happened. Snake couldn't be sure, but he thought it had gone on for weeks, maybe even months.

And the Looks. They could be anywhere — at the supper table, watching TV, shooting baskets — and suddenly Snake would glance up at Glenn and see a cloud cross his face. Glenn's smile would vanish, his eyes would glaze over, and he would — disappear. Into his own, private world.

Suddenly it dawned on Snake what it was that was different about Glenn now: the Looks. He didn't get them anymore.

Snake rolled onto his side. He felt surprisingly calm. For the first time in ages, he knew what he had to do.

Chapter 24

The next morning Snake got up early and went out for a run around the neighbourhood. It was a beautiful, almost-spring morning. The sky was bright and a warm breeze blew through his hair.

When he reached home, he showered quickly and changed into his school clothes, taking a moment to study his body in the mirror.

Wow. Was this the same body he'd peered at with distaste in the fall? Snake flexed his arm muscles, then his leg muscles. There they were, clearly defined, one-hundred-per-cent genuine muscles. Even his freckles seemed to have faded.

He walked downstairs.

His mom and dad were both in the kitchen, eating breakfast. For a moment, Snake's sense of calm vanished. He shuffled into the kitchen and sat down, greeting his parents in a shaky voice. He poured himself a bowl of cornflakes and dug in, glancing up now and then at his parents. His dad was doing some last-minute marking of his students' assignments, and his mother was reading the paper.

It can wait till tomorrow, Snake tried to tell himself. But he knew that if he waited till tomorrow, he'd keep putting it off. It's now or never, he thought.

Snake took a deep breath.

"Mom? Dad?" he said. They both looked up. "I need to talk to you."

His mother breathed a sigh of relief. "Thank God," she said. "You haven't talked to us in months."

"What's this about?" asked his dad.

Snake swallowed hard. "I've spoken with Glenn."

Pause.

"You phoned him?" his dad said finally.

"Uh, huh."

"Why?"

"I missed him," he said.

His mother looked at his father. "Of course. It's only natural."

"Did he see things our way?" his dad asked, leaning forward, a glimmer of hope in his eyes.

"No," Snake said. "He's not going to, either."

"How do you know that from one phone

call?" his dad asked.

He took a deep breath. "Because I didn't just talk to him. I visited him."

The room fell silent. His parents stared at him.

"You *what?*" his dad said quietly.

"This weekend. When I told you I was staying with Joey. I went to London, instead."

His dad's face turned a bright shade of red. "How could you lie to us?"

"I knew if I told you, you wouldn't let me go."

Snake waited. He knew what was coming. His dad would blow up now. He would jump up and pace back and forth, waving his arms frantically as he yelled at him. Then he would ground him.

But he was wrong.

"You're right," his dad mumbled. "We wouldn't have let you." He leaned back in his chair and stared down at the palms of his hands.

"He misses you guys so much," Snake told them.

"I miss him, too," his mom murmured. "And I know you miss him, Reggie, even if you won't admit it," she continued, looking straight at her husband. "He's still our son, and I still love him. And we want him to be happy, don't we? Isn't that all that really matters?"

"It's not that easy," his dad said.

"No," she agreed. "But that doesn't mean we can ignore it, either."

She reached out and put her arm around her husband, caressing his head like he was a small child.

Snake looked at the clock on the wall behind his parents. "Mom, Dad. I've got to go or I'll be late for school."

"Go ahead," his mom said. "Your father and I have some things to discuss in private, anyway."

Well, thought Snake as he got up to leave the kitchen, that was surprisingly easy. But as he reached the doorway, his dad called out to him, "We'll talk about this more at dinner, young man. The fact is, you lied to us — "

"I know, and I — "

"Don't interrupt me when I'm talking," his dad said sternly. "You're grounded. For two weeks."

Snake sighed as he left the house. Oh, well, he thought. It could have been a lot worse.

All through English class, Snake watched him. When the bell rang, he leaped from his seat and stood by the door, waiting.

Alonzo took his time gathering his books together. When he finally reached the door, Snake made his move.

"We need to talk," he said.

Alonzo gazed at him with barely disguised disgust. "I don't think so," he said, brushing past him.

Snake followed him down the hall.

"All right," he said. "I'll talk. All you need to do is listen."

Alonzo didn't even turn around. He stared straight ahead and continued walking down the hall.

"Remember," Snake began, "remember the question you asked me last time we spoke?"

Alonzo didn't respond. He stopped at his locker and fiddled with the combination.

"Do you?"

Alonzo still didn't reply. But Snake thought he saw him nod imperceptibly as he yanked open his locker.

"I wanted to let you know ... the answer is yes."

Alonzo's hand froze in mid-motion. He still didn't turn around.

"I would still be your friend."

Slowly, Alonzo turned around and looked at Snake. His expression was stony and his eyes betrayed nothing.

"Yes, I would still be your friend."

Alonzo's stony gaze wavered ever-so-slightly.

"That's all I wanted to say," Snake said.

He squeezed Alonzo's shoulder. Then he turned and strode down the hall.

Chapter 25

A few weeks later Snake sat in history class, fidgeting while the teacher handed out their marked test papers.

The sports awards banquet was in a week. Snake knew that if he wanted to go, he had to order tickets by the end of the day.

He couldn't make up his mind. Each player was allowed to bring three guests, and the custom was that you brought your parents and a date.

The parents weren't a problem. But the date definitely was.

He'd heard all the other guys from the team talk during lunch about who they were bringing. BLT was bringing Michelle; Luke had a date from another school. Snake had learned from them that Tom was bringing Tamara and bragging loudly that he was a shoo-in for the Most Valuable Player award.

Just the thought of Tom made Snake shudder. Ever since the night at the purple building over a month ago, Snake had avoided him and his friends like the plague. If he saw him in the hallway, he turned and walked the other way. If he saw him in the cafeteria, he took his lunch and ate it by his locker.

No, he thought now. It would be better not to go at all than to show up without a date.

"Good work, Snake," the history teacher said now as he laid Snake's paper facedown on his desk. "This is the kind of work I know you can do."

Snake flipped over the paper.

A large red *A* stared up at him.

"All right!" he whispered. The bell rang. Snake gathered his books together then bounced into the corridor. As he got closer to his locker, he could see that someone was leaning against it.

Tamara.

"Hi, Snake," she smiled.

"... Hi."

Wow. For the first time since he'd known her, his heart hadn't skipped a beat when she spoke to him. He started to open his locker.

"Your hair's red," he said.

"Yeah. I henna'ed it. You like it?"

Snake shrugged. "Sure."

Tamara started to twist a few strands of her brand-new red locks between her fingers. "You liked the blonde better, right?" she said doubtfully. "Maybe I should bleach it out."

"It looks fine. Besides, if you like it, that's all that matters, right?"

"I guess," she replied, clearly unconvinced. "I mean, I did it 'cause supposedly it's the latest thing. At least, that's what the fashion mags say," she went on, trying to laugh.

Snake looked at her for a moment. *Really* looked at her. We have more in common than I ever realized, he thought. She's just as insecure as I am.

"Listen, I was wondering," she was saying, "the sports banquet is coming up and I'd really like to go … "

"What about Tom? Isn't he kind of your boyfriend?"

"Not any more, he isn't," she said, wrinkling her nose. "He can be such a jerk sometimes."

"Really? I hadn't noticed."

If she heard the sarcasm in his voice, she didn't show it. "I thought maybe I could be your date for the sports banquet?" she said.

Snake looked at her. She still looked the same as ever, even with her red hair, yet for some reason Snake didn't think she looked so beautiful any more.

A while ago, he would have jumped at the chance. And it was still tempting. Very tempting. Imagine showing up at the banquet with Tamara Hastings on his arm ... The looks he'd get from the other guys ... The looks he'd get from Tom ...

"So? What do you say?" she said, her voice wavering slightly.

As gently as he could, he said, "Thanks for asking. Really. But I don't think so."

Her eyes widened, and Snake could see her bottom lip tremble. "Why not?"

Good question, he thought. Why not?

Then it dawned on him. He knew why he couldn't bring Tamara. He had the perfect excuse.

"Because," he told her, "I already have a date."

Chapter 26

The gym was crowded with people. Tables had been pushed together in long rows in the centre of the gym, with chairs on either side. On another wall stood the buffet table, and Snake could smell the aroma of roast beef waft through the air.

On the wall opposite the buffet stood the awards table. Behind it stood a stack of stereo equipment. When the ceremony was over, Snake knew that the DJ would set up his equipment, and the party would really begin.

As he wandered toward some of his teammates, he ran a hand along the fabric of his suit. His mom and dad had taken him out shopping for it yesterday after he'd tried to squeeze into his old suit without success. The new suit was navy blue, and it hung loosely and comfortably on his limbs.

Underneath his suit jacket was the shirt

Glenn had given him for Christmas. He'd dug it out of his drawer this morning and ironed it. It was a perfect fit, and the cotton fabric felt smooth and cool against his skin. "Hey, Snake!" BLT slapped him on the back when he saw him. "Good to see you."

Snake smiled. "Good to see you, too," he said. He greeted Luke, who was drinking pop from a styrofoam cup beside BLT.

"Nice suit," another voice said.

Snake looked up to see Alonzo. "It's new," he replied.

"It looks really good on you," Alonzo said, looking Snake directly in the eye to show that he meant it.

Snake smiled. "Thanks. You look good, too."

"As always," Alonzo joked, and the other guys laughed.

"Hey, fellas!" Snake looked up to see Tom Schenk push his way into their circle. Behind him came Bob, Marco, and Tamara. She eyed Snake coolly.

"Guys, you all know Tamara," Tom said, his chest swelling like a proud rooster.

They murmured hello.

"Hey, Alontho," Tom said when he saw him. "How'th it going?" He held up a limp wrist and waved it in Alonzo's direction.

"Shut up," Snake said.

Tom looked up in surprise. "What did you say?"

Snake took a deep breath. "I said, shut up."

For a split second, Tom faltered. "Oh, right," he said now, laughing, "I forgot Alonzo was your boyfriend."

"You are such a jerk," Snake continued, the anger rising in his throat. "You're an ignorant — mean — jerk." He spat each word out separately. His body was tense with months of stored-up anger.

The other guys — even Alonzo — were shocked into silence.

Bob and Marco moved to either side of Tom. Tom's eyes narrowed into tiny slits. He poked Snake's chest with his finger. "Take it back, Simpson. Take it back now, or I'll beat the crap out of you."

Snake didn't flinch. He slapped Tom's finger away from his chest. "Don't touch me."

Tom clenched his fists. "Take it back."

"No."

"Take — it — back," Tom said, gritting his teeth.

"No."

Snake's mind was racing. You can beat me to a pulp like you did to that guy last month and I won't take it back, he said over and over in his head. His insides were shaking, but outwardly he tried to look calm. "We've listened to your crap long enough," he heard himself say. "I'm sick of it."

Tom clenched his fist and kept it clenched. He took a step backward, drew his arm back —

Suddenly, BLT stepped in front of him and grabbed his arm in mid-swing. "I don't know about the rest of you guys, but I think Snake's right. I'm sick of your dumb remarks, too."

Tom stared at BLT in disbelief.

"Ditto," Luke said, standing on the other side of Snake.

Tom's eyes darted from one face to another. He tried to laugh. "Come on, guys. I was only joking."

"But it's not funny," Snake said.

"Man, what's wrong with you guys?" Tom said, clearly shaken. "You take everything too serious." He took Tamara's arm. "Come on. Let's go sit down."

The two of them strode away, with Bob and Marco following close behind.

"Way to go, Snake," said BLT. "I've never liked that guy."

Snake's limbs started to relax. He noticed that his knees were shaking.

Alonzo patted him on the back. "I'm not going to say thank you," he said, "because I know you didn't do it for me. You did it for you."

Snake nodded.

"Besides," said Alonzo, "I can look after myself.

Snake laughed. "I know you can."

"So, who's your date tonight?" asked Luke, changing the subject.

"I don't really have one," Snake admitted. "I brought someone else instead. Someone I think you guys would really like to meet."

"Who?"

"Follow me."

Snake led the way to his table. "This is my mom," he said, "and this is my dad. And this," he said, "is my brother, Glenn."

"Glenn Simpson!" BLT almost yelled. "Man, could we have used you to show us a thing or two earlier this year."

Glenn laughed. "I hear you guys did pretty well without my help."

"How long are you in town?" asked Luke.

"Just over the weekend."

"If you have any time, you have to show us some moves."

"That's up to my brother, I guess," said Glenn, looking at Snake.

"Sure," said Snake. "Sounds good to me."

"Would everyone please take their seats," announced Mr. Raditch, who was MC for the evening.

"See you after the ceremony," said BLT

as they hurried to find their seats.

Snake sat down beside Glenn.

"I'd love to come," Glenn had said when Snake phoned. "But what about Mom and Dad?"

"Mom thinks it's a great idea."

"And Dad?"

"Dad ... isn't thrilled. But Mom kind of insisted that he make an effort."

"Oh."

"It won't be an easy weekend. You know Dad."

"Oh, well. At least it's a start."

Glenn had arrived last evening. Dinner had been tense, but at least no arguments had broken out. After dinner, they'd watched a ball game on TV, and everyone had seemed a bit more relaxed.

Later that night, when they lay in bed — Glenn over by the window, Snake by the door, just like it had been when Glenn had been living at home — Snake spoke into the darkness.

"How did you know?"

"Hmm?"

"That you were gay?"

"I didn't know for a long time. But I've felt different ever since I was seven."

"Seven?"

"I had a crush on Josh Oppenheim."

"Really?"

Glenn laughed. "Really. Then, in high

school, I had other crushes. They terrified me. So I dated as many girls as I possibly could."

"But how could you fake enjoying ... being with them?"

"I didn't have to fake. I did enjoy it. But I just knew it wasn't me. I liked women a lot, but I loved men. In grade twelve, I fell in love for the first time."

"With who?"

"Remember Allan Jackson?"

"Allan Jackson? No way!"

They both fell silent for a moment.

"Glenn?"

"Yeah?"

"Would someone my age know by now?"

"Not necessarily. Some people don't come out till they're a lot older. And some people never come to terms with it. Why?"

"Sometimes I ... I'm really attracted to girls ... But sometimes I feel attracted to guys ... "

"It's natural to have those feelings, whether you're gay or straight," Glenn said. "The important thing is being happy and being yourself. And in your case, whoever that turns out to be, I'm pretty sure I'm going to like him."

They fell silent again, for a longer time, and Snake started to worry that Glenn had drifted off to sleep.

"Glenn?"

"Mmm?" he answered sleepily.

"Do you ever worry? About the way some people treat you?"

"I used to."

"I worry. I've read a lot of stories in the paper. I worry you're going to get beaten up, or worse," he said, picturing the young guy in his head.

"I can't worry about those things. I just have to live my life as who I am. I'd rather be out and happy than miserable and in the closet."

"What about AIDS?"

"Condoms, Arch. Don't they teach you in school that it isn't just a gay disease? When you start having sex, promise me you'll use condoms."

"I promise."

"Good. I've got to sleep now. I'm exhausted."

"Good night."

"Night."

Snake stared up at the ceiling for a moment, his mind still buzzing.

"Glenn?"

"Mmm?" he mumbled.

"I like Greg."

"You've got good taste."

"Glenn?"

"Mmm?"

"I'm glad you're home."

"Me, too."

"Arch, this is your category," Glenn nudged him.

"... The winner of the Degrassi Boys' Basketball Team Most Valuable Player Award is ... " Mr. Raditch was saying.

Snake looked up.

" ... Archie Simpson, better known as Snake."

For a moment, Snake didn't budge from his seat. A great cheer rose from the tables where his friends sat.

"Go!" Glenn laughed, giving Snake a push.

Snake felt like he was floating on a cloud as he walked up to the table and picked up his award. He glanced around the room and saw rows of faces smiling at him.

Except for Tom. He sat pouting at his table.

When he sat back down, his mother threw her arms around him and hugged him. "I'm so proud of you, Archie. I'm so proud of both my boys," she said.

"Congratulations, son," his dad said, extending his hand. Snake took it, and they shook.

The DJ had started to set up his equipment. "I think we'll pass on the dance," his mom said. "We're going to go home and talk."

"Sure."

"You going to be okay here on your own, kid?" asked Glenn.

"I think so. There's someone I've been meaning to talk to." He hugged his mom and his dad, then Glenn. "It's thanks to you that I won this award," he said to Glenn.

"No, it isn't," said Glenn. "It's thanks to you. You're the one who had to do all the hard work."

"See you at home," Snake waved as they walked away.

When they were gone, Snake surveyed the gym.

Then he saw her.

He ambled over to where she was standing, talking to some friends. Her hair was down tonight, and she was wearing a dress, and Snake found himself thinking, she's pretty. She's really pretty.

"Hi, Melanie."

"Snake," she said, arching her eyebrows in surprise.

"Congratulations on your swimming award."

"Congratulations to you, too."

Snake stared down at his feet, suddenly feeling tongue-tied. "I know I've been a jerk," he said. "And there's lots of things I'd like to tell you — "

He stopped.

"Here," he said, reaching into his pocket and handing her something.

"What's this?"

"Open it."

She tore off the paper to reveal a book.

"*The Tin Flute*," she said, reading the title aloud.

"I hope you haven't read it already."

"No. I haven't."

"I read it last month. It's really good. Depressing, but good."

Melanie's cheeks were flushed. "Thanks. Thanks a lot."

"It's — kind of a belated Christmas gift," he said, looking down at his feet.

"Christmas in May! What a great idea," she giggled.

For a moment, they didn't say anything.

"I was wondering," Snake said, "if maybe you'd like to dance?"

Melanie smiled. "I'd love to."

As they wound their way to the dance floor, a slow song ended and a fast song began. Snake hesitated. But Melanie started to jump around and get into the music right away. Snake shuffled his feet back and forth awkwardly. Then the music started to seep into his bones. He felt good. Terrific, even.

He felt his limbs loosen up, and he started to move to the rhythm. His arms started to swing, and his long legs twisted and bounced along with the music. His whole body started to move, and out of the corner of his eye he could see that some people were watching him, some of them smiling, some of them laughing.

And he realized he didn't give a damn what anybody thought.